A Home for Barney

Pride Pet Play

Elouise East

Contents

Author Note

If you would like to see any potential triggers for this book and any other books I've written, please go to this link on my website: https://elouiseeast.com/triggers

One

LIAM

L iam Sawyer entered The Den with only a slight shimmer of trepidation, leftover from when he'd been beaten by a man who had been a member there. It had happened over a year ago, but that tremor as he crossed the threshold had been there ever since. Even knowing the man, Vincent, was now in prison for trying to blackmail and kill a member of the royal family, not to mention other things. How Liam got entwined with the man, he didn't know. It just happened one day when he didn't have a handler to take care of him during his pup time.

He signed in at the reception desk within the foyer, ignoring the bass pounding through his bones, and headed to the stairs to the side of the bar. The Den had two floors. The main floor was a basic club with dancing, a DJ and smaller sectioned-off areas for the voyeuristic and exhibitionists. The upper floor was where the more diverse club members went. It held everything else from age play to bondage play to pet play, which was Liam's wheelhouse. Unfortunately, he had no handler, which meant he had to play alone and take care of himself unless there was an eligible handler available.

And by eligible handler, he meant someone willing to be his handler for the evening. Sometimes, a handler who already had a pup or two would allow him to join them, giving him a better experience. Other times, there was a handler with no pups at all. His friend Robert had been that to many pups before he found his partner. Robert had also been the person to help Liam get away from Vincent that night, and they had become firm friends afterwards. Robert and Henry, who just happened to be a prince, were getting married in a couple of weeks, and they had invited Liam to celebrate with them. He couldn't wait.

But that night, he needed to breathe, and to do that, he needed to be a pup. Barney was his pup name, and he wore a brown and white neoprene suit that had gloves, shoes and a mask that turned him into Barney when he needed to let the world fall away.

On the upper floor, the music was quieter, but the moans and groans of ecstasy were louder. Liam glanced around to see who was present and was pleased to see Dodo, a brown pup he sometimes played with, and Nomad, a mischievous black and white pup. They both had handlers, but they were fun to play with.

Barney could get rambunctious sometimes, and Dodo and Nomad were just as bad.

Nomad saw him and came scrambling across the floor to bash into his legs, nearly sending Liam flying. He laughed and patted the pup on the head.

"I'll be there in a minute, Nomad. Go play!"

Nomad nudged his face into Liam's thigh and bounded off, back to the mosh pit, almost colliding with another pup. Liam shook his head and grinned. Heading for the small bar at the back of the room, he ordered water, slid his custom-made name tag around the neck and placed it on the counter to the side. He could come back and get a drink when he needed one without coming out of pup space too much. He found it jarring to slip from pup space to normal to pup space again, so he tried to mitigate that as much as possible.

Slipping on his shoes and mask first, he then slid on his gloves and presented himself to no one in particular while he relaxed into being Barney. It didn't take long when he concentrated on the pups' yips and growls. He watched a handler throw a ball, which came in his direction, and he focused on it. It rolled to the side, and he sprang after it, nudging it with his nose and sending it in a different direction. Another pup came up beside him, trying to get it, but Barney nosed the ball away again, and they both raced after it. Barney overshot the mark, and the other pup yipped but jumped back when the ball squeaked at him. Laughter sounded, and Barney chased the ball and the pup back to the mosh pit.

He stopped in front of Dodo, pressing his chest to the floor and wagging his tail, wanting to play, but Dodo's handler said, "He's just having a rest, Barney. He'll play again in a bit."

Barney whined but turned to the other pups. Another pup had joined, and Barney yipped and raced over. This pup was all black and sleek, but Barney knew him. Barney pounced forward and back, getting closer to Dusty each time, trying to entice him to play, but Dusty sat beside his handler until Robert said, "Go play, Dusty."

Dusty knocked into Barney and sent him flying, but Barney got his feet back under him and chased after him. Robert threw another ball for them, which sent all the pups into a tailspin. After several long minutes, Barney panted hard and trotted over to the table. He removed his gloves so he could reach for his drink. But his drink wasn't there.

"Barney! Here, boy!"

His head whipped around at his name, and he dashed towards Robert. "That's it. Good boy. I brought your drink over to us so you can have some company. Here you go," Robert said, holding out his bottle of water with a straw poking out of the top.

Barney drank, closing his eyes and letting the cool liquid soothe his warm body. When he pulled his head away, Robert patted him, then placed a bowl of treats on the floor. Barney devoured the savoury cheese crackers—his favourite—then had another drink before heading back off to play again.

He wasn't sure how long he played for, but he'd been called back to Robert twice more. The next time, Robert told him he and Dusty were heading home, and Barney whined.

"I know, Barney. We'll find someone for you as soon as we can."

Dusty pressed against his side, and Barney nudged his head in thanks. He was difficult, that was the problem. Feeling himself slipping out of pup space, Liam pulled off his gloves and mask and settled on his ass on the floor, sighing.

"Thank you, Robert. I appreciate it. And thank you for tonight. I didn't realise how much I needed to let go until you took over."

Robert smiled. "I know it's difficult when you're on your own, but you know you're welcome to ask if you ever need this. We won't leave you without someone. There are plenty of people we know who could do this for you."

Liam nodded. "I know. It's just..." He swallowed and looked away.

"I understand. Not everyone is like him, Liam. I promise you that." Robert looked around. "There's just a decided lack of handlers in this place." He frowned at someone, and Liam glanced in that direction, seeing a guy turning away from them. Who was that? He turned back when Robert started talking again. "I don't know why because despite how unkempt and seedy this place looks, it's one of the better ones."

Dusty finished his drink and rested his head against Robert's leg. Robert rubbed his back, and Liam pushed away the jealousy wanting to bubble up. It was his own fault he didn't have a handler. It wasn't like he hadn't been asked before, but after Vincent, he just couldn't let go enough to give someone control. Someone who wasn't a friend, that was.

"Are you heading home now, Liam?" Robert asked.

He nodded. "Yeah. I've had the breather I needed, thanks."

"You're welcome. You know that."

Liam reached to scritch Dusty's ear, and the pup pushed into his hand. "Thank you for sharing your handler, Dusty."

Dusty didn't come out of pup space until he'd had a nap usually, but Liam hadn't seen him take one. Either he had and Liam hadn't seen, or he was going without that night. The pup trusted Robert to make sure nothing happened to him during that time, but Liam would never allow himself to be so unaware, even with someone he trusted, like Robert. Liam stood and thanked them again before heading for the stairs. He wanted to get home, showered and into bed before the calm of his pup play left him completely. It didn't last as long as it used to, which meant he had to visit more often to keep the level head he needed to have to think straight.

He signed out and drove home, ignoring the longing voice in the back of his head telling him he needed more. He might need more, but he couldn't get it, and he had to live with the tumultuous thoughts every day.

He parked in the residents' car park for his apartment building and let himself into the building with his key fob.

Forgoing the lift—he wasn't keen on small spaces—he ran up the ten sets of steps to the fifth floor, panting when he pushed through the door to the corridor. His apartment was one of four on the fifth floor, but the furthest away from the stairs. He passed three doors, two on his left and one on his right, then unlocked the last door on his right and stepped into his living room. Locking it behind him, he rested back against it for a second.

A beep echoed through the room, and he sighed and strode over to the answer machine. He knew who the voicemail would be from, though why she used his home phone and not his mobile, he could never understand—even when she explained it.

"Hi, Liam! It's Lora. I'm assuming you're out, as you didn't answer. Unless you've decided to ignore me for once. Nothing much to say except I can't wait until this baby is out! How can I still have four weeks to go? It's so not fair that the women have to deal with this." She sighed. "Anyway, are you coming over next weekend for dinner? You usually do, but I wanted to check. Call me tomorrow, okay? Love you."

The answer machine beeped, and he left the message on there. It would remind him to call her in the morning, though he didn't plan to make it too early. It was a Bank Holiday, which meant he could sleep in. He never booked jobs for those days because people were always taking off to the beach or something, thinking the weather would hold out for them, but it rarely did. For some reason, the weather thought it was hilarious to rain on almost every

Bank Holiday the U.K. had. Didn't matter if it was the height of summer, either. It still rained.

That was the other reason for not booking jobs. Being a landscaper wasn't pleasant when the weather didn't cooperate. Business had just picked up again now spring had arrived, and he was booked for weeks to come.

He wandered to his bathroom and unfastened and dragged off his pup suit, putting it to one side to remind him to clean properly before he next wore it. He had several identical suits, so it wasn't urgent, but he always looked after his things. He switched on the shower and climbed in straight away, allowing the pinpricks of cold to hit him before it warmed up enough to be soothing. Scrubbing away the sweat, he let his mind drift, allowing the calming of his pup play time to sink into him. He'd visit The Den again the following day, as it was his day off, and give himself another night of freedom before locking it all away until the following weekend.

· · • ● · ● · ● · • · ·

He didn't sleep in as long as he wanted, thanks to his sister. The phone rang, and he stumbled from the bed to answer with his eyes barely open and his brain misfiring. That had to be the reason he agreed to meet his sister for brunch, rather than going back to bed.

He hung up and groaned, rubbing the grittiness from his eyes. Yawning, he stumbled to the bathroom and showered in cold water, needing the spikes of ice to wake him up completely. When he was shivering enough to make a bowl of jelly tremble in his hands, he climbed out and dried off. Dressing in jeans and a T-shirt with a picture of a Labrador puppy and the quote, "*Handle every stressful situation like a dog. If you can't eat or play with it, pee on it and walk away.*" It was one of his favourites, and he had plenty of them. He collected them, weird as that might be.

He shoved his arms into a hoodie he probably wouldn't keep on for long, pulled the sleeves to his elbows, slipped his wallet, keys and phone into his jeans' pockets and left the building.

He walked the twenty minutes to Book Drunk, Lora's favourite cafe and bookshop. It was owned by the boyfriend of another prince, Christian, and although Liam had never met the prince, he'd spoken several times to Oscar. He had a feeling Oscar was a little or a pup or something along those lines, but he would never ask; it wasn't polite to do so outside of a club. Plus, it wasn't his business. All he cared about that morning was the breakfast Lora said she'd treat him to.

Entering the cafe to the tinkling of the bell above the door, he searched for a redheaded, tiny person, also known as his sister. She'd snagged her favourite table by the window so she could people-watch while indulging in her decaf coffee and cake love—decaf only because she was pregnant.

She beamed at him as he drew closer, and he leaned down and kissed her cheek.

"Good morning, sunshine. How's you and the baby?" he asked, settling opposite her.

She rubbed her stomach, the small beach ball sized bump making it more difficult for her to sit close to the table. "We're both good. I'll be happy when I can start drinking full-strength coffee again, though. They're great here because they make the decaf drinks as nice as the non-decaf ones, but there's something about that caffeine hit…" She chuckled.

Liam snorted. "I would've thought you would've got over your addiction by now. You've not had much caffeine for how long now?" He knew how long, but he wanted to distract her.

She groaned, dropping her head back and pouting. "Don't remind me it's been twenty-seven weeks. And counting. I can't count the first nine weeks because I didn't know."

Liam swallowed his chuckle. "Anyway, where's my food?"

Lora glared at him. "I don't mind paying, but I wasn't ordering it until you got here. You might've fallen back to sleep."

Liam shook his head, smiling. "Do you want anything?"

Lora pursed her lips and shook her head. "I'm good."

She didn't sound good. Liam joined the queue and decided on a full English breakfast and a latte to start his day. He ordered Lora a white chocolate and raspberry muffin because, although she said she was good, she would never turn down one of those. He grabbed the latte and the muffin and carried them back to her, sliding the plate in front of her. She gasped and clasped her hands to her chest.

"Thank you!" She grabbed a fork from the pot on the table and dug in.

Liam sipped his latte and watched, waiting for her to inhale it before they returned to their conversation.

"Of course I'll be there next week. It's on Sunday, right?" he teased, knowing full well it wasn't.

She threw a balled-up napkin at him. "You know very well it's on Saturday, so don't be mean." He held up his hands in surrender.

"I'll be there," he said seriously. "You know I will."

Lora smiled at him, and despite their ten-year age gap, he felt closer to her than he had been to anyone else. Ever. They'd grown ever closer since their parents' death eight years ago. Liam had taken over Lora's care. Even though she'd been eighteen and able to stand on her own two feet, he'd been there to support her. It was only when she sat him down and told him to stop hovering that he travelled the country, trying to find who and what he was. It was on one of those stops that he'd found himself in a kink club and been introduced to pups. He'd never looked back. His sister had no clue about his kink lifestyle, and he was happy to keep it that way.

But now, he was back in his hometown of Windsor, and he was trying to put down more roots, especially now Lora was pregnant and bringing the next Sawyer into the world. Although the baby would be a Montgomery, not a Sawyer, but same difference.

"Here you go. One full English breakfast," Oscar said, sliding the plate in front of Liam.

"Thanks. How are you?"

Oscar grinned. "I'm very well, thank you. Are you having a good Bank Holiday?"

"We are, thanks. I was surprised you were open," Lora said.

Oscar chuckled. "I thought my customers would need me more than Christian would today. Enjoy."

Oscar wandered off. How did the man keep his feet on the ground when he was with a prince? Liam expected some people would've thrown it in others' faces regularly. But not Oscar. He spoke of him as if he was a normal, everyday person. Which highlighted exactly how down-to-earth the royals of this generation were. If he hadn't met Henry, he wouldn't have believed it.

"Are you excited about the wedding?" Lora said, keeping her voice low.

Liam rolled his eyes. "It's a wedding. It'll be nice to see them get married, but I'm uneasy with how high-profile it is."

"You'll be on TV!"

Liam snorted. "If you can find me amongst the five hundred guests, if not more, then I'll buy you muffins for a month."

"Deal."

Two

Troy

Troy Robson couldn't keep his eyes off the pup, and it made him feel a bit like a creeper. He'd first seen the brown and white pup a couple of months ago and laughed at his mischievous actions with two of his pup pals. Two of them had handlers who reined them in occasionally; the other didn't from what he had seen. The pup, Barney, came and went alone, and the loneliness on the man's face was apparent, even to Troy, who struggled to interpret the emotions of other people. He was too shy to ask how people were feeling, so he had to rely on his not-so-great instincts.

But he was sure this pup was one he would get along with, although he couldn't bring himself to approach him. Instead, he leaned against the walls of the club, like a stalker, watching Barney's antics and nursing his drink.

So far, he'd worked himself up three times to talk to the man—Liam, he believed his name was—and each time he walked past him to the stairs, Toby opened his mouth but nothing came out. Afterwards, he slunk home and hibernated until he found himself back in the same spot, trying to gather the courage to talk.

It wasn't that he couldn't talk to strangers. He did so every day as an estate agent, but this was different. This was...important.

He used to have no problem approaching a potential pup to see if they wanted a handler, either for a night or for longer. But after being burnt several times—once by a guy who had cleaned out his house of anything valuable—he was more careful and withdrawn. He hadn't made the first move towards a pup for about a year; he relied on pups coming to him. But there was something about Barney—Liam.

And that's what brought him back time after time.

Liam stood and grabbed his drink from the table he'd put it on. Troy had been monitoring it to make sure no one messed with it. Even from across the dimly lit room, he saw the sweat slicking Liam's curls to his face when he removed his mask, and his Adam's apple bobbed as he drank. Troy tried to avert his gaze, but he couldn't. Liam was mesmerising, both the man and the pup.

Liam capped his bottle and strode towards him. Well, towards the stairs. A black and white pup intervened, stopping in front of him, and Liam chuckled.

"I'll be back at the weekend, Nomad. Go. Have fun."

Nomad pushed his head into Liam's hand, then scampered back to the mosh pit. Liam watched with a small smile and then headed Troy's way again. Troy shifted, staring right at him. His stomach churned, and he opened his mouth when Liam was a few steps away. The words disappeared when Liam glanced at him. His mouth curved, and he nodded once, then he descended the stairs. Troy's shoulders dropped, and he banged his head back against the wall repeatedly.

"Fuck's sake, Troy," he murmured.

He pushed away from the wall and threw his bottle in the bin. Following in Liam's wake, he cursed himself for not being brave enough to try. Yes, he'd been burnt, but surely, one day, he would have better luck.

He'd been attending The Den for about a year now, after having to find a new club where his previous pups weren't members. He couldn't face seeing them and knowing what they'd done to him and might do to others. He'd heard of the exclusive Club Royal but didn't even try, doubting they would find him suitable. Well, actually, they might have, considering who his sister was, but he refused to link himself to her, especially when it came to his kinks. He could just imagine the screaming matches that would cause between him and his family. Anything that shone a less-than-stellar light on Gina was unacceptable.

He stopped beside his car and pinched the bridge of his nose, sighing heavily.

"Everything okay?"

Troy whirled around, slamming his hand against his car when his feet tangled together. "What?" His sole word was garbled, and his heart appeared to be trying to pound out of his chest.

"Are you okay? You look a little out of sorts," Liam said from inside his van. It made him almost the same height as Troy was. He had the window wound down and had his phone in his hand.

"Uh-huh." Troy cleared his throat, took a breath and said, "Yes, I'm okay, thanks."

"Are you sure? That sigh sounded like it carried the weight of the world in it."

Troy tried not to concentrate on the fact that they were having their first conversation and his lungs didn't want to work, and instead, formed words to answer him.

"It was that bad?" he croaked.

Liam's eyes crinkled as he smiled. "Worse possibly."

Troy leaned back against his car, needing to stop his knees from collapsing him to the ground. "I must be in a bad way, then."

Liam chuckled. "Are you sure you're okay?"

Troy nodded. "Just been a long year."

"It's only May."

"Exactly."

Liam cocked his head like Troy had seen him do as Barney. "You like to watch the pups."

It wasn't a question, but Troy tensed. Was Liam setting him up for an argument? "I'm a handler, and I love watching them."

Liam's eyebrows rose. "I've never seen you play."

Troy shrugged. "I don't have a pup."

"There are plenty there who wouldn't mind having a handler for a night."

Troy nodded but didn't reply. It was the truth, but what other reason could he give for not wanting to play without giving too much away?

Liam's phone chimed, and he broke their staring match to check his screen. He smiled, then glanced at Troy again. "If you're sure you're good, I have to go."

Troy didn't want the conversation to end, but he couldn't hold Liam indefinitely. "Thanks for checking on me."

"You're welcome. Have a good evening, Troy."

Liam pulled out of the car park, and it was only as his heart returned to its usual beat while he sat in his car that he realised Liam had used his name—and Troy had never even given it to him.

• • • ● • ● • ● • • •

"Yes, Mrs Martin. They dropped off the keys this morning. All you need to do is come and fetch them, and the house is yours."

"But I can't get there yet. Can't you bring them to me?"

Troy kept his sigh silent and closed his eyes. "I'm afraid I can't. But we'll keep the keys for as long as you need."

"Fine."

Mrs Martin ended the call without a goodbye, and Troy replaced the receiver while rubbing at his forehead. Some clients were never happy. Even if he did acrobatics while holding a tray of one hundred full crystal champagne glasses without spilling a drop.

"Troy, I can't find the folder for the Grover Place house," Nate said. He had been working this job as long as Troy had, but for some reason, he couldn't get his head around the computers, no matter how many times he'd been shown.

Troy wandered over to Nate's desk, leaning down and rescuing the mouse from Nate's clutches. "Have the mice hidden from you again?" he joked.

Nate snorted. "When don't they?"

Troy clicked a few icons and brought up the file for him. "There you go. Is someone interested?" He leaned his hip against the desk and crossed his arms.

Nate nodded. "They called a few minutes ago and want to view it."

"Do they know the state of the place?"

Nate raised a shoulder. "Seemed to. Said they were looking for a place to do up and sell on."

Troy grimaced. "It might be more work than they're thinking it will be. The place needs gutting."

"True, but maybe I can sway them and get the property off our hands."

"If anyone can, you can, you sweet talker." Troy grinned and jerked back as Nate swiped at him. He returned to his desk, dropping into his chair with a sigh.

"What's got into your bonnet, anyway?" Nate asked. "You've been sighing and huffing all day."

"I'm worn out."

"You've just had a long weekend. How can you be worn out?"

Troy glared at him. "I meant worn out from life, Nate. Not work."

"You're only, what, forty? How can you be worn out at your age? You wait until you get to my age, then tell me about being worn out." Nate shuddered.

Troy didn't correct the age guess because Nate was only out by a year. At thirty-nine years old, Troy was not bothered at all about ageing. He welcomed every year he was on the planet, except he wanted someone to share it with. Alone, it was long and tedious. With someone he cared about, he expected it to be long and exciting.

"You're still going strong though, Nate. That says something," Troy said.

"Yeah, that the government has increased the retirement age again so I can't retire yet." Nate wasn't wrong, but he was nowhere near retirement age yet. He might have thinning hair, a beer gut that he blamed on takeaway rather than beer and arthritis, but he still had plenty of years left.

Troy chuckled. "The retirement age will have increased by ten years by the time I even get close to it. I can almost guarantee it."

"Probably."

Troy's phone rang, and he inhaled before picking it up. "Good morning, Hartley Estate Agents. Troy speaking. How can I help?"

And so the day went. Enquiry after viewing after enquiry after viewing. He loved his job, but some days, it was monotonous. When he finished at five-thirty that afternoon, he had never been more grateful for working a nine-to-five job. That the week was only four days was a bonus. He couldn't wait to get back to the club that weekend to see if he could build on his conversation with Liam if he was there.

As he drove home, the radio newsreader spoke of the upcoming royal wedding. Prince Henry was marrying a commoner, and everyone seemed divided about whether or not they agreed. Some groups were protesting him marrying a man, some were arguing he shouldn't be blending his DNA with a commoner, and some were celebrating the union as a step in the right direction for gay rights. Troy thought the prince should marry who he wants to and forget about everyone else. Which seemed to be what he was doing, and with the full backing of the royal family.

When a song he didn't recognise came on, his mind wandered back to Liam, as it had done every hour since Liam had driven away the previous evening. He wasn't sure whether Liam would continue to talk to Troy should they cross paths again, but he needed to figure out what he could say should it happen.

He pulled into his driveway, no closer to an answer, grateful he had large trees hiding him from his neighbours. He spoke to them in passing, of course, but he kept to himself more than anything. His parents had bought him a house "in keeping with their status," to ensure he didn't disappoint them with his choice, but the five-bedroomed detached house was far too big for just him, despite how enormous his aquarium was.

As he closed the front door behind him, his shoulders released the tension plaguing him. He hung up his jacket, kicked off his shoes and stared at rugs he still hated. His mother, Mila, had chosen them for him, but the multi-coloured monstrosities covered too much of the beautiful wooden floor for his liking. He sighed and ignored them, as he always did, and headed right into his office. He set his briefcase on his desk and strode for the aquarium that filled the entire length of the back wall.

He'd been fascinated with animals from a young age, but fish and turtles had become his favourite. The one thing he had splashed out on was an aquarium big enough to hold his turtles and fish. They were so soothing to watch at any time of day or night if he needed a breather. He'd been caring for turtles for fifteen years now and had learnt many lessons along the way.

He fed them, then headed for the kitchen to feed himself. Staring into the fridge didn't find anything that had miraculously made itself; therefore, he grabbed a pack of bacon, some spaghetti and cheese, and started on spaghetti carbonara. While the pasta cooked, he flicked the TV on, selecting the series he was currently working his way through. NCIS had been recommended to him, amongst others, and he was slowly getting through each episode. It kept the quiet away.

While he ate, he finished the episode, then shut it off, placing his plates in the dishwasher. He wandered through the rooms until he reached what he called his den. It was the smallest room of the house, but he'd set it up with a sofa, a TV, a stereo, a chair, a music stand and, most importantly, his flute.

None of his family knew he played, and that was perfectly all right with him. Gina had enough talent for them to throw at the world without them leaning on him, too. He didn't want to be in her place, not even a little. Her piano playing was elite—the best of the best—and he didn't begrudge her that, but he did begrudge his parents showering Gina with everything she could possibly need and pushing Troy into the background as if he wasn't needed, or worse, didn't exist.

He settled himself into the chair and reached for the instrument, running his hands over the metal keys as he did every time before he played. He'd picked up the instrument for the first time when he was ten years old. His school had brought different instruments into the classroom so they could try them and see if they liked any. The school had been trying to get parents to pay for lessons. When Troy had heard and touched the flute, he'd known. But he refused to ask his parents. Instead, he'd spoken with his teacher, who happened to be a flute player himself, and Mr Royce had given him secret lessons after school twice a week.

Since then, he'd never looked back. And despite Mr Royce no longer being with him, he still remembered every lesson he gave. But he still refused to share his love of playing with anyone else. They would not place him in front of a thousand people to make money from. Gina did that enough for the both of them.

He licked his lips and brought the flute to his lips, positioning his fingers automatically. He closed his eyes and ran through some scales to warm up. When he finished, he slid right into his favourite song, *Perfect* by Ed Sheeran. From there, he went through several songs, including one he had just started trying to master. After an hour, he cleaned his flute and put it back away again, his body thrumming with energy. He took himself to his home gym and pushed himself on the treadmill before showering and settling into bed with a book and a glass of red wine.

As he sipped the wine, he closed his eyes. Despite the day being long and arduous, he was as relaxed as he could ever get. Liam's smile filtered into his mind, and Troy smiled in response. He was such a handsome man and, undoubtedly, a handful of a pup. If he ever had the chance of looking after him, he wouldn't be bored, that was for certain. He knew a little about Liam, but Troy wanted more. He wanted to know what made Liam tick, what made his pup so different from the sense he got of Liam as a man. Maybe this weekend would be the one Troy would pluck up the courage to start the conversation.

He would love to play with Barney, but until he'd spoken to Liam more first, he wasn't comfortable approaching the pup. He didn't know why when he'd done so with other pups in the past. What made it different that it was Liam? Had the damage those previous pups made hurt him enough to stay alone for the rest of his life? That was something he had to work through. And preferably before the weekend.

He was shy; he knew that, but before he'd been burnt, he'd never had a problem before. He needed to get back to that way of thinking. He knew he was living differently from before because of his experiences, which was to be expected. The thought of those past relationships stopping him from starting a new one was an unsettling one.

Troy tilted his head, ear to shoulder on each side, cracking his neck, then picked up his book and opened it where his bookmark waited. Soon, he lost himself in a different world, where werewolves could scent who belonged to them, and it made life that little easier.

Three

LIAM

When Liam signed in at The Den that Friday, the receptionist gave him a leaflet, and he waited until he'd climbed the stairs to the upper floor before he looked at it. He expected it to be a sale or something, but what he didn't expect was to see Elton requesting volunteers to be part of a Pride event.

From what he could gather as he read, Elton was putting on a taster session for various kinks every Saturday during Pride month, the "tamer" of which would be part of the Windsor Pride Festival parade on 17 June. Liam's eyebrows rose at the "Windsor" part of it. Why wasn't Elton taking part in the Slough Festival instead? He might ask if he saw the man. But colour Liam intrigued by the information. Spending every Saturday playing as a pup with handlers to keep them in line sounded fantastic.

The leaflet said to complete the form if anyone was interested. Liam went to the bar, ordered his drink and asked to borrow a pen. He filled it out there and handed it to the bartender to give to Elton.

Who would be the handlers and how many handlers and pups would there be? If there were too many, it could become a nightmare, but Liam was sure Elton had thought of everything. He seemed organised enough, but this was the first event of its kind from Liam's knowledge.

He drank some water before placing the bottle on the table. Glancing around the room, he saw the usual people, and he hoped the event might bring some new people into the lifestyle, or at least let them know The Den wasn't as bad as it appeared from the outside. He truly wished Elton would do something about that neon flashing sign at the very least.

"Have you signed up for the event?"

The voice made Liam's mouth curve, but he schooled his expression before facing Troy. He appeared to be quieter than most members, keeping to himself.

"I have. I'm hoping it might bring more people here. There's a need for more handlers."

Troy nodded. "I've seen that."

Liam cocked his head. "Are you joining in tonight?"

Troy scrunched his nose and stared at the floor as he fidgeted. "I don't think so."

"How come?"

He didn't answer Liam's question straight away, but then his gaze flicked up to Liam's. "I'm not staying for long tonight."

The blue of his eyes, which seemed brighter than he remembered them being the last time he saw him, mesmerised Liam. He nodded. "Have you signed up for the event?"

Troy cleared his throat. "Not yet. But I think I might. It'll be a nice way to celebrate Pride."

"It will." Liam peered down when something—or someone—nudged his thigh and chuckled. "Okay, okay. I'm coming," he told Dodo. The brown pup dashed back to the pit, and Liam smiled across at Troy. "Have a good evening."

He pulled down his mask, though he didn't miss the way Troy stared at him as he did. He pulled on one glove, but before he could struggle with the second one, Troy was there, helping. When Liam was ready, he dropped to his knees and nudged his head into Troy's hand as a thank you. Troy petted him, scratching his ears, and then Barney bounded off, losing himself in the chasing game.

When Barney stopped for a drink, Troy was nowhere to be found, and he told himself he wasn't upset about that.

· · · ● · ● · ● · · ·

Liam concentrated on placing the rocks where they needed to be to keep the new pond from folding in on itself, ignoring the need to stretch his muscles until he finished. He stood, reaching his arms above his head to remove the kinks from his spine. He pulled his T-shirt back into place, smoothing a hand over that day's quote, *"If my dog doesn't like you, I probably won't."* It was so true. Although Liam didn't have a dog himself, he thinks of Barney whenever he sees shirts like that.

"Liam, dear! Would you like a cup of tea and a biscuit?" Mrs Corrigan asked. She was always trying to fill him up.

"That would be lovely, thank you!" he called back.

Mrs Corrigan was a widow, who loved fish, and she had decided to have a pond put in her back garden so she could see them every day. Liam didn't know the first thing about looking after fish, but he knew how to install a pond. It was part of his job, after all. When the pond was full of water and the decorative stones in place, it would look fantastic. She'd requested a small tree to be placed at the back of the pond, like a backdrop to the picturesque look, with the pond in front and purple and white stones surrounding it and the tree. It would be in the shape of the number eight when he finished. In theory, anyway.

"Here you go, dear."

Liam strode towards the back door and took the mug from her hands. "Thank you." He slurped the boiling brew and closed his eyes, sighing. "Perfect." She held out a plate with chocolate digestives on it, and he took one. "You certainly know how to look after me."

"Few people can decline tea and a biscuit. Especially if they're British," she said, slipping into the rocking chair on her back porch. The porch Liam had built for them last year. Before Mr Corrigan passed away. She waved him towards the second rocking chair, but he hesitated. She smiled. "Donald wouldn't mind, Liam. It's just a chair."

Liam settled into the comfortable seat and sighed, wishing he had one of them for himself. It wouldn't be much use at his apartment, though.

"It's a beautiful day," Mrs Corrigan said, smiling.

"It is."

They drank in silence, but Liam should've known it wouldn't last long. "So, Liam, why don't you have a partner yet? Time's awastin'." She clucked her tongue.

Liam chuckled. "I'm happy on my own at the moment."

"Codswallop! You have the same look about you that my Michael did before he found his wife. Try again."

Liam shook his head, smiling at her words and looking at his tea as if it could tell him the right thing to do. "I was hurt, Mrs Corrigan. I'm slowly finding my way back."

"People only make you feel inferior if you let them. Eleanor Roosevelt said that."

"She did. And that's why it's taking me so long. I knew better. I'm getting there, though." He tried to sound optimistic.

"Glad to hear it."

They spoke for a few more minutes—and he was grateful she stayed away from relationships—before he thanked her for the break and went back to work. He hoped he would finish the pond that day, and then the following day, he could concentrate on the decorative stones.

Mrs Corrigan's words had taken hold, and he couldn't get the idea that he was running out of time from his mind. It was a silly idea because he was only thirty-six. It wasn't like he didn't have a few more years before he was over the hill. While he worked, he contemplated why he wasn't joining a different club if The Den wasn't giving him what he wanted. When he'd not found what he needed at the other clubs around the country, he'd moved on. Windsor was his hometown, but The Den wasn't the local club. Why did he keep going back? Especially when that was where he'd been beaten.

An image flickered through his mind, and he paused in his work, leaning his forearms on his knees and staring into the pond as it filled with water. There was no way he was staying for Troy. He'd only met the man a week ago. *Not true.* Liam sighed as his brain argued with him. It was true. He'd only *met* the man a week ago, but it wasn't the first time he'd *noticed* him. When he'd originally seen Troy nine months ago, Liam had been wary, for obvious reasons. He'd pushed aside any inclinations towards a permanent handler because he had no idea who he could trust. Every time he saw Troy after that, he'd ignored everything about him. *Not true.*

Liam sighed and rubbed his hand over his clenched jaw. He'd tried to ignore everything about him, but he couldn't help soaking up whatever he heard through the gossip mill, which wasn't much. He still wasn't sure who he could trust, though, and that was the worst thing of all. He wanted to have a relationship—a handler and pup relationship, too—but he couldn't let himself go enough to reach for it.

He strode to the outdoor tap and switched off the hose. After checking the pond to make sure it seemed to do what it should do, which was holding the water without leaking it anywhere, he grabbed all his tools and set them in his wheelbarrow, pushing it down the side of the house. He piled it into his van and closed the doors before heading back to let Mrs Corrigan know he was leaving for the day.

When he got home and was showered and making his dinner, his mind wandered to the Pride event again. There was no date for when Elton would let them know if he had chosen them for the event, but he assumed it would be sooner rather than later because people would need to make plans. How was the event going to work? Would they be on a float, or would they be walking around? It would be fantastic if they could use a float and make a small mosh pit because it would mean the pups got less tired and could last longer at the event.

He wasn't organising it, though, so he had no say in it. He also assumed Elton would allocate them a handler if they didn't have one. Or would Elton choose those pups who had a handler already? Liam's stomach rolled. That would probably be the wisest choice, but he would miss out if that was the case.

His mind whirled and swirled with thoughts and questions that had no answers yet until the timer on the oven beeped. He pulled out the shepherd's pie and plated one portion, the rest to be saved for the coming days. Having an enormous appetite was a nightmare for cooking meals sometimes. He usually had two portions of what a normal person would eat as one of his portions. Cooking larger quantities was the only way to make sure he didn't have to cook every day. He didn't mind cooking, but it wasn't his favourite.

His phone pinged just as he sat on the sofa. He leaned to one side to pull it from his jeans' pocket.

VAL: *Tell me you're not eating alone again.*

LIAM: *I won't tell you then.*

VAL: *Liam! You're supposed to be getting yourself out there. Mingling. Finding true love, and all that jazz. Stop making me do all the work.*

LIAM: *And what work are you doing?*

VAL: *Cheerleading, of course. Can't you see my pom-poms?*

LIAM: *Idiot. We're two hundred miles away from each other.*

VAL: *They're metaphorical pom-poms.*

Liam chuckled even as he shoved more food into his mouth. Val Tomlin had been his best friend since they were kids. He'd been a year ahead of Liam in school, but they'd lived around the corner from one another and became fast friends. Unfortunately, Val decided to go to university in Edinburgh, and he'd fallen in love and made a home there with his boyfriend, now husband, Adam. Liam had stayed with them for a few weeks during his travels, but he couldn't settle, and Val knew it. He called him on it while he'd been there, and Liam had finally spilt the beans about everything that had happened. It was therapeutic in a way.

LIAM: *I will, Val. I will. There's an event the club is putting on. It might be fun.*

VAL: *Liam Sawyer wants to have fun? Where did my un-fun best friend go?*

LIAM: *I'm still here, but I'm taking your advice. I'm getting out there. Or at least, I'm trying.*

VAL: *Good. I'll call at the weekend, and you can tell me everything. I have so many things to share...*

LIAM: *Fuck off. You know I hate it when you do that!*

VAL: *You can wait six days. It's not going to kill you.*

LIAM: *You're only waiting until Sunday because you want me to spill about the wedding.*

VAL: *Hell, yeah! I never, in all my wildest dreams, thought I'd be friends with someone who would attend a royal wedding. It's nuts.*

LIAM: *Bye.*

VAL: *Hey! You know I love you.*

LIAM: *But you love the royal family more.*

VAL: *...maybe. But I love you, too.*

LIAM: *I know. I love you, too. Speak to you later.*

Val was a ball crusher when it came to getting Liam to do what he told him to, but he meant well. He truly wanted Liam to find his other half so they could both live happily ever after, and since the incident with Vincent, Val had been trying even harder. Liam could understand it, but it didn't make it any easier for Liam to trust.

His phone pinged again.

VAL: *Don't forget to get your suit cleaned.*

Liam chuckled. Val didn't have to worry about that. Liam hadn't wanted to let Robert and Henry down, so he'd bought a new suit that sparkled and waited to be worn. The wedding was fast approaching, and he was nervous—not that he'd let anyone else know that. As much as he joked with Val and Lora that they wouldn't be able to find him while searching the TV screen, it was mind-blowing to think they'd be trying. Whoever tuned in to watch the royal wedding, however much smaller it was than the one planned for Prince Frederick in a few months' time, would have the chance of seeing Liam there. Anyone around the world would be able to see him.

He finished his meal and washed his dishes. He didn't see the point in using a dishwasher when there was only him and he barely used any plates. As he settled into bed after his usual night-time routine, his thoughts travelled to the Pride event again. There was a butterfly sensation in his stomach, and he realised it was excitement. He wanted to take part, even if he would potentially, once again, be on TV. He wanted to be part of what Elton created to show Windsor—or the country or the world—what Pride meant to them. To show them what was out there. What they could do or be.

Liam hadn't been given much support as a teen, and Pride meant a lot to him. He wanted to spread that support as far and wide as he was able. Being only one person, it wasn't that far, but if he could help just one person, he'd be elated.

Everything the king was doing to support his children had overwhelmed Liam with the strength of the man—taking on the world for his children was beyond Liam's comprehension, but the thought behind it was immense. If Liam ever had children, he hoped he could be as strong as the king was. He'd fight off lions if it meant his children could be who they wanted to be.

But that was far into the future. Liam frowned. Or maybe not too far if he wanted to keep up with young kids. He was thirty-six already. Too much longer and he'd be too old for kids. And what if the man he gave his heart to didn't want them? Could he live without a family? He could, but he wasn't sure he wanted to. He wanted to shower children with love and cherish them as they grew. Liam sighed. That would have to go on his list of questions to ask potential partners. He didn't want them to decline further down the line.

Potential partners? What was Liam doing? He hadn't thought about finding anyone more than a handler for months. For some pups, a handler was just that. Someone who looked after them while they were pups. For others, a handler was their life partner, being the other half of their heart all day, every day. He shook his head on his pillow and closed his eyes. Val's words must've pierced deeper than Liam had realised.

Liam rolled onto his back and stared up at the darkened ceiling. Could he consider finding someone to spend his life with? The idea wasn't as painful as it had been months earlier, and when Liam pushed to see who he viewed as a person he might consider getting to know, the only person who came to mind was Troy.

The man seemed so unsure, and Liam wasn't certain he could be the handler he needed. After all, Barney was a handful. He would need someone who could deal with Barney and Liam's uncertainties. Could Troy be that person? Liam wasn't sure at all. But it wouldn't hurt to find out more about him. Especially if Troy took part in the taster events.

Yes. If Troy took part in the taster sessions, Liam could try him out as a handler and see if they were compatible before throwing himself all in. Which sounded bad when he thought about it in those terms. He wasn't interviewing the man. He needed to be sure they could work before he took the chance of losing his heart.

That was one thing he hadn't worried about with Vincent. There had been something about him that Liam had instinctively known, and he would never have lost his heart to the man. Even when Vincent had his kind moments, there was always something lurking in the background. Why Liam had let it go as far as it did, he didn't know. He was immensely grateful to Robert for his part in helping Liam get away, even if he ended up with injuries from it.

He rubbed a hand over his ribs. He'd had three bruised ribs and one fractured, which had taken far too long to heal, but he'd survived. He couldn't lose sight of his instincts because that was what kept Liam from losing himself completely to Vincent, and that was what would ultimately help him choose the best partner for himself.

He just had to believe in himself and decide he wanted to try. Which was easier said than done.

Four

Troy

T roy had been on the fence about whether to sign up for the event. It was the reason he'd approached Liam in the first place that night, especially as it gave him a topic to open the conversation without him fumbling around for something to say. When Liam confirmed he'd signed up, Troy knew he would sign up, too. Even if there was only a slim chance of him being partnered with Liam, he had to try. He didn't know Elton well enough to request it, and anyway, Elton might think him a weirdo—and not in the good sense.

If he was chosen and was partnered with someone else, he'd deal with it. But if he was selected with Liam... Well, that would be fate.

The only slight rumble in his plan was his family. If Troy took part in the event, there was a chance his parents would see or be told that he was in it. He didn't look forward to having that conversation, but as they were in Australia at that moment, there wasn't a huge amount they could do until they returned in six weeks.

He hoped.

He wrapped a towel around his waist after showering, and his phone chimed. Exiting the bathroom to retrieve it from where it was plugged in on his bedside table, his heart rate doubled when he saw the message was from The Den.

Congratulations and thank you. The Den invites you to take part in the Windsor Pride Festival. We would like you to be available every Saturday in June from noon until two o'clock. You are also free to attend the taster sessions outside of those hours should you wish. As you do not have a pup/partner that we are aware of, we have allocated a pup for you. If you already have a partner, please let us know as soon as possible. Please could you confirm you're still willing to take part in the event and advise if you can attend an information session on Friday, 12 June at three o'clock? Thank you once again. Elton.

Troy stared at the message as he sank onto the bed, his legs trembling and unable to hold him up any longer. He had a momentary *"What the fuck am I doing!"* thought, and then he rubbed his hand over his forehead and exhaled to calm himself. This was what he wanted. To get more involved with the community and to face his shyness head-on. He refused to think about being in front of however many thousands of people who would be at the festival, cheering and shouting for those in it.

Elton had allocated a pup to him. Who? He hoped it was someone he at least had a little knowledge of. Surely, they would meet up beforehand... He glanced at the message again. They wanted them to attend an information session. They'd probably tell them who they were with there, so he could meet them. They were, after all, going to be handler and pup for a while.

He typed out a reply, confirming his attendance and his lack of a pup, and thanked him for the opportunity. Then he dropped backwards and stared at the ceiling. Was this the right choice?

Two days later, he was still asking himself the same question as he entered The Den at two-fifty-three on Friday afternoon. He'd requested the afternoon off work, apologising for the short notice, but his boss agreed without hesitation. He sometimes wondered if the man knew who Troy was related to, which was why he gave him such leeway with things. He didn't want special treatment, but if it got him this afternoon off, he wasn't complaining.

The Den looked completely different with the lights fully brightened and no music. Chairs had been set up in three rows of six in front of a booth towards the back of the room. There was a table off to his left with drinks and snacks, and his feet took him in that direction straight away. He grabbed a bottle of water and checked out who else was there while he unscrewed the lid and took a swig. He recognised some faces, and some were new, but there were only ten of them, eleven including him, and the seats accounted for eighteen people. There were still people to arrive, then.

Choosing a seat on the back row at the end and scooting the chair back a little so others could slide past him, he sat sideways and crossed his legs. He rested his bottle on his knee and his elbow on the back of the chair next to him, his chin leaning on his fist as his gaze took in everything around him. He might not be the first to join a conversation, but he enjoyed watching people and being nosey.

More members trickled in. Including Liam. Troy licked his lip as Liam tracked across the floor, smiling and waving to other people. His gaze landed on Troy, and Troy could see him hesitate before heading over to him.

"Hey, I have to admit to thinking you wouldn't sign up," Liam said when he stopped beside him.

Troy chuckled. "It was a very vigorous debate in my mind, let me tell you."

Liam smiled and waved to the seat next to him. "Is this taken?"

Troy's heart pounded so hard he thought it would escape his chest. "No, not at all."

Instead of walking around the other side of Troy, Liam dragged the chair out of the row, stepped in front of it and pulled it back again, their knees bumping as he settled himself into the groaning seat. Liam wasn't a small man, and the chair knew it. Troy couldn't look away from the play of muscles beneath his grey T-shirt. There was a smudge of something on the sleeve, a similar colour to what was on his jeans and boots.

"You didn't have any problems getting time off work?" Liam asked, breaking Troy's focus.

Troy blinked, his brain coming back online, and shook his head. "My boss was very kind. It's not like I haven't done enough overtime to warrant it." He chuckled.

"What do you do?"

"I'm an estate agent."

Liam raised his eyebrows, a small smile playing around his lips. "Really. I'm a landscaper."

"Not too different then," Troy joked, trying to play it cool, although his stomach was in knots and his palms sweated.

"Well, I've worked for several people who were getting their houses ready for selling. We might be closer than you think." Liam covered his mouth, hiding the smile.

Troy shook his head and sighed. "Small world."

"Good afternoon, everyone. Thank you for being here at such short notice," Elton interrupted from the front of the chairs. The bulky, muscular man had sat on the booth table, making himself a little taller so everyone could easily see him. "So, you are the chosen ones." He paused with a smile when chuckles ran through the room. "Couldn't resist, sorry. Okay. First, I'm going to go through the plans for the taster sessions and let those of you just doing that know who you'll be with. After that, you guys can leave if you want to. Then I'll explain the festival. At the end, those of you who don't have a pup or handler partner will find out about your Pride Festival collaborator. Does that sound okay?"

Troy saw people nodding, and Elton clapped his hands. "Brilliant." He explained about the taster sessions, which were happening every Saturday in June from four o'clock in the afternoon. Troy might attend some, even if it was just for moral support.

"I understand not everyone is going to be at the taster sessions," Elton continued, "but I wanted you to have the information in case you wanted to join in. Those of you who are doing just the taster sessions, here are your partners."

Troy watched as several of the newly made couples shook hands, grabbed a sheet from Elton and headed out.

"Let's hope the festival is as easy," Liam murmured.

Troy snorted but didn't reply as Elton started talking again. "This year, Windsor Pride Festival organisers have changed things up a bit. In previous years, our sector was part of the walking procession through the town centre. This year, they've given us two floats, plus some walking room between them."

Liam shook his fist on his lap in celebration, a smile crossing his face. Why was he happy about that?

"This means you can rotate from walking to the floats if you need to rest. The floats themselves will be mosh pit style, but you'll be safe, I promise."

Elton continued, and the more he spoke, the more Troy's stomach rebelled about being in front of so many people. He wasn't sure if he could do it.

"Questions so far?" The man answered some questions, but Troy zoned out a little.

"Are you okay?" Liam whispered, leaning close enough that his cologne wafted towards Troy.

Troy closed his eyes, inhaling deeply, and nodded. "Yes, thanks."

"You look a little pale. Are you sure?"

Troy cleared his throat. "I'm pretty shy, as you know, and the idea of being up on the float scares the hell out of me."

Liam jerked back a little, staring Troy in the eyes. "Why did you sign up then?"

Troy could hardly tell him the reason, especially as he didn't know who he was partnered with yet. He shrugged instead. "Broadening my horizons?"

Liam squinted at him but said nothing.

"All right, then. Let's get into your partnering. Those who already have partners and have confirmed this, you know who you are already. The rest of you... Handler Eliot with pup Wanda. Handler Gemma with kitty Buttons. Handler James with bunny Fluffy. Handler Kian with kitty Fudge. Handler Troy with pup Barney. Handler—"

That was all Troy heard. His mouth gaped as he transferred his gaze to Liam's. Liam winked at him. "Guess we're going to get to know one another more, after all."

Holy crap.

He had hoped, but he never truly believed Elton would pair him with Liam. Now what did he do?

"We can change partners if you want to," Liam said, and it was the uncertainty in his voice that snapped Troy from his fugue state.

"No!" He glanced around, ducking his head when people glanced over at them. "No," he said quieter. "I'd like to stay with you if that's okay with you." He winced at his terrible use of English, but Liam was lucky Troy could talk at all.

Liam scratched his head and then smiled. "I'm happy. We've got time to practise. Not that we need to, of course. We could just wing it on the day. It's not essential."

Troy's mouth twitched at the flow of words speeding from Liam's mouth. He wasn't the only nervous one. "A practice run would be good."

"Brilliant. Are you busy tonight? I can't do tomorrow."

Troy winced. "I can't do tonight. What about next weekend? Saturday?"

Liam narrowed his eyes and tilted his head in what Troy assumed was a thinking pose because, a few seconds later, he nodded and straightened up again. "Yes. Next Saturday would be great."

"Perfect. Is six o'clock too early?"

"No, that's fine by me."

They stared at each other, grinning at their date—no, not a date. Practice run. It was just a practice run.

"Okay. If no one has any other questions, you're free to go."

Troy glanced at Liam. "What did we miss?"

Liam winced and shrugged. "No idea. Oops."

Troy snorted, the sound bursting out of him. "That seems like something Barney would say if he talked."

Liam laughed, holding his stomach and bending forward. The deep vibration made Troy smile wider. "So, so true. You've got your work cut out for you, Troy. Barney can be mischievous when he wants to be."

"You don't say." Troy bit his lip, trying to contain his smile again. He checked his watch. As much as he wanted to stay and talk to Liam some more, he had to meet up with his best friend. "I'm sorry, but I have to head out."

Liam stood, nodding. "It's okay. I won't be staying now, and to be honest, I shouldn't come back tonight. I've got a busy day ahead of me tomorrow. I need my beauty sleep."

"Do you work weekends?" he asked as they headed for the door, clutching the sheets of paper Elton had handed to them with a smile and a roll of his eyes. The man had obviously caught their lack of attention.

"Usually, yes. But I have a wedding to attend tomorrow."

"Oh, wonderful. I hope you had a good day."

Liam blew out a breath. "It'll be a day, put it that way."

Troy frowned. "Are you not looking forward to it?" he asked when they arrived at Liam's car.

Liam scrunched his nose and glanced around them. "I am. It's just a big affair, and I prefer smaller ones."

Troy nodded. "I know what you mean. Too many people."

"Too right."

They stood, smiling at each other for a few long seconds, and Troy didn't want it to end. But it had to. "I'm sorry we can't catch up today."

"Me, too. But I'll see you next week. Oh!" Liam pulled his phone from his pocket. "Is it okay if I take your number? Just in case something happens and I can't get here. I doubt that'll happen, but I wouldn't want you thinking I stood you up."

Troy inhaled through his nose, trying to calm his heart. "Sure." He read out his number and felt his phone vibrate in his pocket.

"There. You have mine now, too." Liam slid his phone away again and smiled, unlocking his car. "Have a good evening. And week."

"You, too. Take care, Liam. And don't let Barney get into too much trouble."

Liam placed a hand on his chest. "As if I would do a thing like that."

They laughed, and Liam climbed in his car as Troy backed towards his own a few spaces down. Liam waved as he pulled out of the space, and Troy waved back before facing his car, leaning his hands on the roof and lowering his head.

"Holy shit," he breathed.

His phone vibrated again, and he pulled it out. He smiled at the message from Liam, which was just a dog emoji, and shook his head at the second message, with more turning up as he stared at the screen.

JAMIE: *Where are you?*
JAMIE: *If you flake on me, I'll be pissed.*
JAMIE: *I know where you live.*
JAMIE: *Get your ass here now.*

JAMIE: I'm surrounded by muscular, sporty men, and you know that's my weakness. If I'm not here when you get here, I've probably lost myself in a sea of testosterone.

Troy laughed and sent a quick message back, saying he was on his way. Jamie Ingram had befriended Troy during their first month at the same college. They were on different courses—Troy was doing business studies, and Jamie was doing music—but for some reason, Jamie had approached Troy in the quad, sat beside him on the picnic table and started talking as if they'd been friends for years. Despite the initial shock, Jamie had grown on him. Like a fungus, Jamie would've said.

By the time he reached the pub they'd agreed to meet at, Troy had been through every bit of his interaction with Liam, looking for clues as to how he really felt about being paired with him. He hoped he liked the idea as much as Troy did.

"Hello, stranger," Jamie said when Troy slid into the chair opposite him. "Fancy seeing you here."

Troy shook his head and sighed. "You need new fodder. That's getting old."

Jamie waved his comment away and leaned forward on his forearms, making the table rock towards him. Trust Jamie to get a wobbly table. "Tell me."

Troy sighed again. "Liam."

Jamie's eyes widened. "You're shitting me! Really? You got the sweet deal without even trying?"

"Who talks like that?"

"I'm trying something new."

"Don't. Just don't."

Jamie stuck his tongue out and rested his chin on his palm. "So... You get the one you wanted." Troy rubbed a hand across his forehead, and Jamie laid his hand on Troy's arm. "It'll be fine, Troy. I'm only messing with you. You should be happy."

"I am, but I'm also worried he'll see how shy and weak I am when he gets to know me."

Jamie sat upright and pointed a finger into Troy's face. "You are not weak! Get that thought out of your head, right now! We've talked about this. That's your parents' voices coming out of your mouth, not yours."

Troy closed his eyes and swallowed hard. He wasn't wrong, but Troy couldn't help it. Spending the first twenty years of his life being micromanaged by his parents to ensure he didn't set a foot wrong while Gina's rise to stardom continued was hard to brush off. Despite having been away from his childhood home for almost another twenty years. It's almost as if he had been programmed.

"You are your own person, Troy. And I'm so happy you got Liam. Maybe he'll be the one to help you break through that shell you wear to keep everyone away."

"Maybe."

Jamie raised his hand to get the server's attention and ordered them more drinks. "Tell me."

So Troy told him everything.

Five

LIAM

The wedding had been both amazing and terrifying, and Liam couldn't deny his pleasure in being there for his friends. There was slightly more pomp and prestige than he would ever need, and that was with it tampered down a lot. He'd been able to speak with Robert and Henry a few times during the day, but the event had gone on for hours, and Liam had been exhausted from being on his best behaviour—which Robert had remarked upon with a grin in the afternoon.

But now it was as if it had happened months ago, not a week. The event—the first royal gay marriage—had been brushed aside as reporters focused on the next big thing, which was the even bigger wedding of the heir to the throne, Prince Frederick, to his best friend, Damon. Liam hadn't had the pleasure of meeting them, but Henry had assured him he would eventually.

It was something he didn't concern himself with because he had more important matters at that moment. Like a practice run with Troy for the Pride event. He wasn't sure they needed a practice run, but he wasn't going to complain about it. Whatever time he got to be Barney was fine by him. He was meeting Troy at The Den so they could go through their rules and expectations that would go on for the entire time they were playing together.

And Liam was excited. He was going to have a permanent handler—at least for the following six weeks.

As he entered the club, his throat dried as usual, and he ignored the shiver of unease, instead looking around to see who he could see. Which was no one because all the people he knew were upstairs. But it helped to settle his nerves as he signed in and headed towards the upper level.

He spotted Troy instantly, and his stomach fluttered, and he couldn't stop the smile creeping across his face. Troy was talking to the bartender and hadn't seen him yet, so it gave Liam the chance to study him. His dark blond hair looked almost brown in the low lights of the room, and his tanned skin held a shimmer as if he was sweating. He wore his leather trousers and jacket well, the material clinging to every inch of him, and nothing was left to the imagination, which Liam appreciated. The crinkles at the corners of his eyes and mouth, when he was amused, were a testament to how much he liked to smile and laugh as far as Liam was concerned. Whether that was true or not was another thing.

But it was his eyes that always caught Liam. The bright blue pierced him, looking at who he was as a person instead of his appearance. And it was focused on him right then.

Liam blinked, smiled and headed towards the man who was going to take care of him.

"Hey," he said when he reached the bar and Troy.

"Hi. How are you?" Troy asked.

Liam nodded. "Good, thanks. Busy, but good."

"The weather has done well this week. I bet you've got a lot done."

"And don't my muscles know about it?" Liam joked.

Troy frowned. "We can reschedule if you're hurting."

Liam waved him away with a chuckle. "It was a joke. I'm fine. But yes, you're right. It has been busy with people wanting things done while the weather held. Unfortunately, I'm only one person."

"Have you considered expanding?" Troy offered him a sealed bottle of water.

"Thanks. Um, I have, but I like working by myself. I hire people to work with me on bigger jobs if I need to, but mostly, I manage by myself. I don't have as much responsibility this way."

Troy tilted his head. "Yeah, I suppose you'd have to deal with wages and insurance and all manner of other things if you have to look after employees."

"Yes. Much simpler if I'm alone."

Troy nodded, and Liam took a drink before Troy spoke again. "So, shall we sit and chat about our expectations before we give this a go?"

Liam covered his mouth in the pretence of wiping it to cover the emerging smile at Troy's uncertainty. For someone who was a Dominant and supposed to take charge, Troy was extremely hesitant. Would they work together? Liam needed someone who could keep him in line, and he wasn't sure Troy could.

"Sure."

Troy led him to a corner of the room where a few armchairs sat. There were different areas in this upper level, including the mosh pit, a swing, a fuck bench, a St Andrew's Cross and beds, all of which could be curtained off individually with the drapes hanging around them.

When they settled, Troy asked, "What do you want from this?"

Taken aback by the straightforward question, Liam settled back in the chair and stared across the space as he thought about his answer. "I want someone to make sure I don't go overboard, which I can do when I'm lost inside Barney. I need someone who won't resort to physical punishments if I do something wrong." Liam huffed. "I don't mean...spanking and stuff like that. I mean actual fists and abuse."

Troy stared at him, body tense, and he wiped at his eyes before answering in a gruff voice. "I will never use my body or words to hurt you in anger. That I promise to the very bottom of my soul."

Liam hadn't realised how worried he had been, and even though he knew words were just that, he had a good feeling about how Troy had worded his response. "Thank you."

"Okay." Troy cleared his throat. "Let's take this one step at a time. I've seen your mischievous tendencies. Are you wanting to curb them or just manage them?"

"Just manage them. I can get overexcited and sometimes don't realise I'm being rough with the other pups."

Troy nodded. "Okay. Do you have something that usually works to do that, or would I be working it out for myself?"

Liam glanced across the room at the mosh pit, where several pups were already rolling around and having fun. "I don't really know. I've had handlers just shout to me before, which makes me realise what I'm doing, but I don't know what else might work."

"I'll figure it out. Don't worry." Troy smiled. "What about sex?"

Troy had said it so easily, but Liam's heart rate increased. He grimaced and looked away again. "Um, I don't..." He wasn't sure how to explain.

Troy leaned forward, lowering his voice. "Nothing you say will make me think less of you, Liam."

Liam studied his expression and sighed, staring at the bottle in his hand. "I don't need sex to be part of it, but my libido does respond when I'm Barney. I'm used to pushing it aside, though. It's not an issue."

"Is it something you want to be part of the relationship? This relationship." Troy waved a hand between them.

Liam closed his eyes. "Maybe."

"We'll return to that another time, then." Troy settled back again. "What is your safe word?"

"Avocado."

Troy smiled. "Why do you think we seem to choose food as safe words?"

The random question had Liam blinking for several seconds before he chuckled. "I have no idea. What's yours?"

Troy raised his eyebrows. "I've never had one." He frowned, tilting his head as he stared at his hands. "Celery," he said suddenly.

Liam chuckled. "Do you not like celery?"

Troy pulled a face, making Liam laugh more. "Who does?"

"Me."

Troy shuddered. "Not when I'm in the room, you don't."

"Is that one of your rules?"

"It is now." Troy grinned. "Talking of rules..."

Liam groaned and dropped his head into his hands. "I shouldn't have reminded you."

"There's nothing excessive, I promise. Rule one is to always use your voice if you want or don't want something. I want no misunderstandings. Rule two is to return to me when I call, even if you're enjoying yourself. Rule three is to sit or lie by my feet when you're not playing. Rule four is...to have fun."

Liam stared at him, waiting for more. "That's it?" he asked when Troy said nothing further.

Troy nodded and shrugged. "I'm easy-going, Liam. I'll add more rules if I need to along the way, but we will always discuss them beforehand. Is there anything you want me to do?"

Liam wasn't sure. He'd always had a long list of rules to contend with when he'd had long-term handlers before. It was a little overwhelming to not have as many rules, which was ridiculous. Why would having fewer rules be more constricting to him?

"I can see your mind whirling a mile a minute. What's wrong?" Troy asked, leaning forward again.

Liam settled into his neutral expression, knowing no one would catch anything from him when he did. He'd perfected it over the years. "I expected more rules, that's all."

Troy narrowed his eyes and leaned back once more, pinching his bottom lip with his finger and thumb. Liam couldn't tell if he'd upset him or if he was just taking Liam's word for it, but either way, the extra space helped.

"Until I know what you need, Liam, I can't give you rules. I can give you the basics that I would want any pup to adhere to, which I have done, but any others, ones that would apply only to you, will need to be figured out along the way."

Liam peered at him, even as he kept his head lowered. He never would've believed this confident man was the same Troy who had become flustered in their interactions before. He was an enigma, and Liam was becoming fascinated by him.

"Okay," he said. "Anything else we need to discuss?"

"The only other thing I would like is for you to wear a collar while we're...together, for want of a better word. Is that a deal breaker?"

Liam swallowed hard, beating back the emotion his eyes wanted to evict. He had never been given a collar, even in those relationships he'd spent more time in. Without looking at Troy, he shook his head.

Troy moved closer again, but this time, Liam's stomach swirled. Anticipation? Excitement? He wasn't sure, but when Troy pulled something from his pocket, Liam's gaze latched onto it. It was stunning. The amber-coloured leather collar looked soft, and it had only one adornment—a stylised 'B' hanging from the front of it. Liam's gaze darted to Troy's face. How had he found one on such short notice?

Troy's cheeks darkened, visible even in the low lighting, and he cleared his throat. "Hopefully, you won't think I'm crazy after this, but I..." He paused, rubbing his thumb over the collar. "I ordered this a few weeks ago." Liam's mouth gaped. "Not for any other reason than I thought you deserved it. With everything you do for the other pups, I thought you needed something. For you. When I was given this opportunity, I considered using my collar, but you deserve to be yourself, even when you have a handler. Hence..." He held up the collar. "If you don't want it, it's okay. It..." He cleared his throat again. "It reminds me of your eyes," he whispered.

Liam's throat had closed, and there was no way he could answer Troy, so he did the only other thing he could think of. He kissed him. It wasn't a kiss that would shame all movie kisses in the world, but it was heartfelt, and Liam kept their lips together for a few seconds longer than necessary before pulling back.

They stared at each other for a long moment, then Troy smiled and held up the collar, raising his eyebrows. Liam nodded, his chin trembling as he tried to contain those pesky emotions trying to overflow.

Troy put his drink down, scooted closer to the edge of his armchair and unfastened the buckle on the collar. He slipped it around Liam's neck and fastened it at the back, running his fingers along the edge of it when he was done. Liam still couldn't speak, but he reached a hand up to it and touched the 'B' gently.

"You're welcome," Troy answered when Liam lifted his gaze to him.

Liam had to swallow a dozen times before he could say anything. But finally, needing to get the words out, he said, "I love it. Thank you."

Troy smiled. "Are you up for a play?"

Liam nodded. He'd brought everything with him. He just needed to put on his mask and gloves. He remembered one question that hadn't been answered. "What do I call you?"

Troy tilted his head. "Troy is fine, or Master, if you'd prefer. I don't stand on ceremony as much as some."

Picking up the mask that he'd placed on the small table beside him, he started pulling it on, and when Troy started helping him, Liam settled in to be cared for. Then Troy helped him pull on his gloves. Before anything else, Troy cupped Liam's jaw, mask and all, and nodded and smiled at him.

"Present," Troy said.

Liam inhaled and exhaled, then slid off the chair to the floor, kneeling by Troy's feet, hands on his thighs. Troy's hand rested against Liam's nape, squeezing gently over and over, and Liam relaxed into it, watching the other pups playing. He hadn't realised he'd slipped into pup space until Master spoke.

"Go play, Barney."

Barney yipped and scampered off, bumping into the armchair as he raced for the other pups. Two pups saw him coming and put their heads down, wagging their tails and bracing for Barney's appearance. He slowed down a little but went barrelling through the pups and into a roll with them. Barking and yipping ensued as he raced around the mosh pit, chasing Dodo and Nomad. Well, chasing Dodo. Nomad scampered beside him.

A whistle sounded, and then a ball came darting across his line of sight. Immediately, he lost interest in chasing Dodo and wanted the ball instead. He caught up to it and slid over the top, twisting around to bat it away again. He resumed following it as it weaved across the floor. Nomad bashed into his side, knocking Barney off his path, and Barney growled at him, shouldering him back.

He continued playing with Dodo and Nomad, plus another pup who was a little shy, before Master shouted to him.

"Barney, heel!"

Barney wanted to ignore the call—he was having fun—and he wavered between staying where he was and heeding his master's call. His head snapped from side to side, but when his master called again, he yipped and scampered towards him.

"Good boy, Barney. Let's have a drink, yeah?"

Barney knelt beside Master, chest heaving, and Master held out a bottle with a straw in it. Barney closed his eyes and drank the cool liquid. Once he'd had his fill, he took a step in the direction of the pups, but Master stopped him with a hand on his head and the rattle of something in a bowl.

"Snack time."

Master placed the shallow bowl on the floor in front of Barney, and Barney dived in, suddenly hungry. It wasn't easy, but the sweet raisins were delicious. The bowl moved across the floor with each small mouthful, and he chased it around to get the final pieces.

"Good boy, Barney," Master said when he finished, holding out the drink again.

Barney drank, then pressed himself into Master's leg, resting his head on his knee and watching the other pups. Master stroked his head, and Barney felt sleepy. His blinks lasted longer until he couldn't keep his eyes open any longer.

He became aware of gentle nudging, rousing him from his nap, and Barney nuzzled into the pillow beneath his head. It was a bit hard. Opening his eyes, he saw pups sprawled out across the mosh pit, and he lifted his head, whining.

"It's okay, Barney."

A hand stroked his head, scratching behind his ear, and Barney sighed and glanced around. Master smiled at him.

"Are you feeling better after your nap?"

Barney whined and rested his head on Master's thigh, letting his eyelids drift shut again.

"Hey, now. It's not sleep time again. Do you want to play some more?"

Barney whined again.

"Okay. Let's get you settled."

Master tugged gently on Barney's collar, and Barney pulled his head away, growling.

"Now, now. I wasn't trying to take it off."

Barney lifted his head, wincing.

"This was why I woke you, Barney. I bet you have a numb bum, don't you?" Master said. "Here, have a drink."

Barney drank, and slowly, he became aware of the surrounding sounds, conversations he could hear, skin against skin, groans and moans, and Liam found himself in the foreground. He finished drinking, then pulled at his gloves. Troy took over, unfastening them, then helped him with his mask. Liam's hair was plastered to his head with sweat, and he had a crick in his neck from how he'd slept, but he was relaxed and sated.

He glanced at Troy. "Thank you."

Troy smiled and helped him onto the sofa he'd chosen when Barney had come out to play. "You're welcome. How are you feeling?" He slipped an arm around Liam's shoulders, holding him close.

"Great. Hot." Liam chuckled.

"I can imagine. You were really going for it with those pups. I didn't think I was going to get you to stop at all."

Liam squinted, trying to read the clock, but couldn't—he needed an eye test. "What time is it?"

"Nearly eleven o'clock."

Liam gasped, staring at Troy. "Why didn't you wake me before?"

Troy settled him back against him. "Why? I didn't have anywhere to be, and you hadn't told me you did. Why not rest? And besides, you only slept for an hour. The rest of the time was playing."

"Still," Liam protested.

Troy held up a hand. "Look, I'll ask you in future if you have a time you need to stop, but unless you do, why not play for as long as you want?"

Liam stared at Troy, getting caught up in the sight of those full lips and the tongue that swiped across the skin, leaving a glistening trail. He wanted to feel his kiss again, but this time, he wanted more. His cock pressed against his suit, wanting freedom, but he couldn't do anything about it yet. He needed to get home first.

Troy cleared his throat. "What do you want to do, Liam?"

Six

Troy

T roy wasn't sure where his confidence had come from, but he couldn't make this decision for Liam. If Liam wanted to take the night further, Troy would be happy to. But if Liam chose to ignore what Troy thought was blossoming between them, that was his choice. Troy hoped he would pick the first, though. He had never been one to get aroused by pups, but the change as Liam returned to himself after losing himself in Barney for a while was sexy as hell.

"Would you like to go for a drink?" Liam asked.

Troy's heart skipped a beat, and he smiled. "I'd love to."

They signed out at reception and headed for their cars, which happened to be parked a few spaces away from each other.

"I'd like to change first," Liam said. "Can I meet you there in half an hour?"

Troy took a chance. "Would you like to come to mine? I have a fully stocked bar, and we can relax and get to know one another more?" His heart pounded.

Liam regarded him with a tilted head and then nodded. "Okay. Give me your address, and I'll be over as soon as I'm changed." Troy rattled it off, unbelieving that Liam had agreed. "I won't be more than half an hour."

Troy saw him to his car, backtracking to his own before he exhaled slowly to calm his heart rate. What had made Liam agree? Was it the offer of relaxing somewhere comfortable, or was it the possibility of more? Troy didn't care, but he let his body calm before he drove home, not wanting to cause an accident when he was so worked up.

He parked in his driveway, fumbled with his keys to unlock the door and glanced around to make sure the place was tidy when he finally got inside. He raced up the stairs to change into something other than his leathers, ducking into the shower for a quick rinse beforehand. He was out of breath once he was done. Unable to keep from staring at the door, he parked himself on the third step of his stairs so he could see it and kept checking his watch.

Time slowed to a crawl, as it always did when he was excited about something. When he heard a car crunching on stones and saw headlights flash through the windowpanes, he stood, wringing his hands. Silence descended again, and he held his breath. A click, a crunch, a slam and more crunches brought Troy a few steps closer to his door, waiting. When the knock came, Troy gasped and held himself still for a moment before stepping closer to open it.

"Hey," he said, barely able to speak.

"Hi," Liam said, flinging his keys around his finger.

It seemed they were both nervous.

"Come on in. What's your poison?" Tyler closed the door behind him, enjoying the way the jeans and T-shirt moulded to Liam's body.

"Well, as I drove, I better go for something non-alcoholic."

"Sure." He headed towards the kitchen, trying to calm down. He could admit to himself that he wanted more from Liam that night, but he would leave whatever happens up to Liam. And if they ended up just having drinks and then Liam leaving, so be it. "I have water, lemonade, apple juice or milk?"

"Lemonade, please."

Troy noticed the quote on Liam's T-shirt and chuckled. "You like dogs outside of the club, too?"

Liam brushed his hand down the shirt that said, "*The smaller the dog, the bigger the personality.*" He nodded. "I do."

"Do you want to sit in here or in the living room?" he asked as he filled two glasses.

"Can I have a tour? This place is amazing."

Troy's chest loosened, and he nodded. "Of course you can." He handed Liam a glass and gestured to the door, noticing he'd removed his shoes without being asked. "Follow me."

He led Liam through the house, answering Liam's questions about the things he saw, and they ended up at the bottom of the stairs half an hour later. Troy wasn't sure if Liam wanted to see the upstairs.

"I'm assuming there's more?" Liam said, staring at the floor, then peering at Troy.

Troy wasn't sure how to interpret the look, but he nodded and headed up the stairs, trying to keep his heart from pounding hard enough to exit his body. He showed him the guest bedrooms, the bathrooms and the small room that led to the attic, then he paused outside of his bedroom.

"This is mine."

Liam licked his lips. "Can I see?" he murmured.

Troy's throat was a desert, but he opened his door and gestured for Liam to enter. He tried to see it from Liam's point of view. The light grey walls usually reflected the sunshine that spent the entire day pointing into the room as it made its way across the sky. But right then, the wall lights illuminated the rest of the space. His king-size bed didn't dominate the room with how big it was, but it had a dark grey headboard with two matching stools at the bottom of the bed. The white covers gave some light to the room. Facing the bed was a wall made from white bricks that held a large flat-screen TV and an enclosed shelf beneath it with the other electronics he had fitted. On the other side of the room were two armchairs and a small table in front of the double doors that led to the balcony.

Liam wandered over to the windows, peering out. "Can people see in here?"

"No. The garden has trees tall enough for privacy."

"It's beautiful, Troy."

Troy exhaled. "Thank you."

Liam faced him and leaned his shoulder against the wall beside the window, staring across the space between them. He could've heard a pin drop on the soft carpet as time stretched forward, but he couldn't bring himself to close the distance. Not without knowing what Liam wanted.

"Troy..."

And that there was the cue he waited for. He rounded the bed in slow steps, placing his glass on the table and reaching for Liam's. When they were out of the way, he stopped in front of Liam, one step away from pressing him back against the bed.

"Yes, Liam?" he murmured, staring into his pup's eyes and seeing the need in them.

"Please."

Troy cupped Liam's cheeks, and Liam's eyelids fluttered. "I'm going to kiss you."

"Please." Liam gripped Troy's T-shirt, and Troy lowered his head, keeping his eyes open for as long as he could before their lips touched.

Troy pressed several short kisses to Liam's mouth, nibbling at his upper lip, then his lower lip before swiping his tongue across the plump mounds. Liam dropped his head back, banging it against the wall, and Troy took the offer of his open mouth to dive inside. The first proper taste of him sent Troy's blood pressure higher and his cock pressing against his zip. He tilted his head, needing to go deeper, take more of what was offered. His hands slipped from Liam's face and around to his ass, squeezing and pulling him closer. Liam's arms slid around Troy's neck, and soon, they were holding each other tightly, their mouths devouring each other as they each tried for the upper hand.

Needing to get Liam on the bed, Troy stepped back, taking Liam with him. He spun them so Liam's back was to the bed and crowded him until his legs touched the bed. Then he pulled away, staring into Liam's eyes while his lungs recovered from lack of air.

"Are you sure?"

Liam's eyes crinkled as he nodded, and Troy took his mouth again, unable to do anything else. He skimmed his hands up Liam's body, taking his T-shirt with him and dragging it over his head. His chest was beautifully tanned from being outside, and Troy's mouth watered to get on him. But Liam distracted him by yanking Troy's T-shirt off. And then they were chest to chest. Troy groaned into Liam's mouth as they scrambled to remove their jeans, their lips bumping, leaving and returning repeatedly. When they were down to their underwear, Troy kissed him again, circling his hips to bump their cocks together.

Liam groaned into his mouth and dug his nails into Troy's side while Troy tangled their tongues. He slid his fingertips into the waistband of Liam's briefs, inching them down bit by bit until he freed his cock. Wrapping his hand around the length, he stroked, and Liam shuddered in his arms. Troy lifted his head, staring into Liam's eyes as he worked him. His pupils dilated even as his eyelids fought to remain open. In the end, Liam dropped his head to Troy's shoulder while Troy brought him closer. Liam's eyes shot open when Troy let him go.

"On the bed," Troy ordered.

Liam kicked out of his briefs and scooted back onto the bed, using his hands and feet, his shaft bobbing with each movement. He braced himself with his forearms behind him and his mouth twitched as his gaze roamed Troy's body. Troy pulled his boxers over his leaking cock, and Liam's eyes widened. He stepped out of them and crawled over Liam's body, making him drop fully to the bed.

Troy kept his body from touching while he asked, "Are you sure, Liam?"

Liam met his gaze. "Perfectly sure."

Troy dropped his lower body, rubbing his cock against Liam's, and lowered to his forearms, caging Liam in. "Top or bottom?"

"Bottom, please," Liam murmured.

Troy rewarded him with another kiss, then pulled away again to grab the lube and a condom from the drawer.

"We don't need—"

"Yes, we do. I haven't had time to reassure you I'm clear, but after this, I will make sure I do. Only then will you make the decision." Troy's words brooked no argument.

Liam stared at him for a moment. "What about me?"

Troy frowned. "You?"

"You need to make sure I'm clear, too."

Troy nodded. "We will. Just not now." He pushed Liam's thighs apart so he could kneel between them and squirted some lube onto his fingers before dropping his head to kiss Liam again. His slick fingers found Liam's pucker while his free hand wrapped around Liam's cock again. Liam slid his legs higher, giving Troy more room to work, and he massaged the hole, stroked his cock and kissed him until his entrance gave way to his finger. He pressed inside with one finger, two, three as he took Liam higher and higher with his mouth.

Liam pushed his head into the bed, groaning. "I can't hold it."

Troy removed his hands, and Liam gritted his teeth. "Yes, you can. You're not coming until I'm inside you."

He grabbed the condom and rolled it down his length, wincing at how much his cock pulsed with each movement. It wouldn't take him long to blow.

"Legs up," he ordered.

Liam caught the back of his thighs and opened himself for Troy's viewing pleasure. The slick hole clenched as if beckoning him, and Troy scooted forward, holding his shaft at that entrance. He held Liam's gaze and waited. Liam frowned after a few seconds, and then a smile twitched at the corners of his mouth. He nodded, and then, only then, did Troy push inside him.

The heat wrapped around Troy's cock, strangling him as he pushed deeper, inch by inch. He breathed through the need to pound into him, to take them both where they wanted to go. He held steady until he rested, balls deep. Slipping his arms under Liam's back, he nestled his face into Liam's neck and breathed until his arousal had dimmed slightly. It wasn't as much as he'd wanted because Liam kept writhing beneath him, but it was enough to stop him from exploding after a few seconds.

Lifting his head, he caught Liam's mouth in another kiss, deepening it further as he withdrew from his channel and slid forward again. He repeated the action several times, his climax simmering beneath the surface and waiting to come barrelling down his spine.

"Yes! Oh, yes! Troy, please!" Liam's chanting was music to Troy's ears, and he increased his speed, bracing on his hands as he slammed deep. Liam's eyelids were hooded, and Troy could feel him reaching for the prize, but Troy wanted to try something. Something that would either help or hurt their tentative new relationship.

Troy withdrew. "Turn over. Hands and knees."

Liam didn't hesitate. Troy settled behind him, smoothing his hands over his skin and following the tan lines across his waist and thighs from where he'd been wearing shorts. He positioned himself at Liam's hole again, pressing forward until he slid home. He braced himself over Liam and paused. He breathed, hoping he wasn't making a mistake.

"Barney?" he whispered. Liam tensed, and Troy soothed him with his kisses on his shoulder. "It's okay. You don't need to be scared."

Liam gasped for air, his body taut enough to break with the wrong move. "I... I..."

"It's okay. Either way, it's okay. It's your choice. Always your choice." He rubbed his lips across Liam's shoulder, waiting for Liam's response.

It seemed like hours before he heard a soft whine. Just one slight note of what he'd heard from the pup. Troy withdrew a little and slid deep again, pausing. Another whine, slightly longer this time.

"Good boy," he whispered. "Your choice."

He rose, gripping Liam's hips and allowing Liam to decide how he would respond. Troy focused on his rhythm as he withdrew and thrust, taking them both higher again after the shock which would've left Liam reeling. Troy hadn't known how he would react, but he'd noticed the arousal Liam had sported when he was Barney. He just hadn't been sure if it was something Liam wanted to bring into the bedroom or not. Leaving the decision completely in Liam's hands now, Troy kept his pace, leaning down now and then to kiss Liam's back. He heard a few more whines, and he was sure that was all he would get.

At least until Liam dropped to his forearms and yipped. Troy could see Liam working his cock, and he increased his pace, slamming deeper with each thrust.

"That's it. You feel so good." He tightened his hold on Liam's hips as his orgasm raced down his spine. "I'm almost there. Come with me."

Liam yowled as his ass clamped down on Troy's cock, sending Troy over the edge. He worked his hips through the orgasm until he was too sensitive and pulled free with a hiss. Resting his head against Liam's back, he panted for a few seconds and then asked, "Are you okay?"

Liam whined, which Troy took to mean he was fine, but he needed to see his eyes to believe him. He helped Liam onto his side and cupped his face, feeling the wetness on it. Was it from sweat or tears?

"Liam, sweetheart? Look at me, please."

It took him a few seconds, but he did, and Troy realised it was tears. "Are you okay? Did I push you too far? Did I hurt you?"

Liam shook his head. "I've never... I didn't think..." He sighed and closed his eyes briefly. "I didn't think anyone would understand," he murmured.

Troy brushed his fingers over Liam's face. "You don't need to separate yourself and Barney as far as some people do unless you want to. You need to listen to your body and do what is right for you. Yes, there are some people out there who would frown upon being even a little of Barney while having sex, but not me. You are both Liam and Barney. It doesn't make you any less of a person to enjoy using Barney's voice or even being Barney while having sex. It certainly doesn't matter to me."

"I've heard people talking about how it's not right, but I can't help how I react."

"You don't have to help it. It might not be wise to do it in the middle of the club in full Barney regalia, but in a bedroom with someone you trust, why not. There are so many kinks out there, no one should throw stones at anything."

Liam sighed. "I don't know."

"And you don't have to right now. I shouldn't have pushed, but it was something I noticed and wanted you to understand that I could be a safe place for you if that's what you wanted. You never have to do anything you don't want to."

"Thank you," he whispered.

Troy pressed a kiss to Liam's forehead. "Let me clean you up." He rose and grabbed a wet cloth from the en suite. He cleaned Liam and himself, then encouraged Liam to slip beneath the covers while he removed the throw that had accepted Liam's release. Then he climbed in beside him. "You're welcome to stay if you'd like to." He paused. "I'd like you to, but there's no pressure."

Liam rolled to face Troy, staring at him for so long that Troy thought he was asleep with his eyes open. "You're nothing like I expected you to be."

Troy snorted. "Is that a good thing?"

"Very. I will admit to wondering how you could be a handler when you didn't seem to be dominant."

Troy nodded. "For some reason, when I become a handler, all my shyness drops away. I know what I need to do and to be. It's easier."

"Easier than what?"

Being second fiddle. "Being me, I guess."

Liam slid closer, resting his head on Troy's shoulder. "As a wise person told me, you need to listen to your body and do what is right for you."

Troy chuckled at his own words being used against him. "Touché." He skimmed his hands up and down Liam's back. "Would you like to stay?"

There was a long moment of silence before a quiet, "Yes," met his ears.

Troy pressed a kiss to Liam's head and sighed. "Good. Now, sleep."

"Yes, Master."

Reaching across to the switch that turned off the bedroom lights, Troy smiled. As the room descended into darkness, he relaxed, hoping to persuade Liam to spend the day with him when they woke. He was sure he could find something to persuade him with.

Seven

LIAM

Liam woke cocooned in warmth, and for a moment, he luxuriated in it. He rubbed his face against the soft pillowcase and sighed, enjoying the heat surrounding him.

Then his brain caught up with his body, and his eyes snapped open. Without moving his head, his gaze took in as much of the room as he could, and it wasn't until he saw the huge TV screen that he remembered where he was and what happened. He closed his eyes again, trying to gear himself up to move, but his brain threw memories from the previous night at him. How he begged Troy to take him. How Troy figured out his secret.

"Stop thinking so hard," Troy mumbled, voice rough with sleep.

Liam tensed, but Troy's hand started petting his stomach, and Liam couldn't find it in him to move away.

"Everything's fine," Troy said. "Nothing to worry about."

Liam wanted to laugh, and a non-humorous one at that. Everything was *not* fine. How could he let himself go like that? How could he make such an ass of himself? Despite Troy's reassurance, Liam couldn't believe that Troy wouldn't turn around and use his actions against him at a later date. This entire event was a colossal mistake, and he should withdraw from it.

"I can imagine what's going through your head right now," Troy said. "But I need you to remember what I said. Everyone has different kinks. Everyone is allowed to do whatever feels right for them. It doesn't matter what others think. And to hopefully put your mind at ease, I have no issues with what we did. None at all. I enjoyed myself immensely. And I hope you did, too."

Liam swallowed and tried to relax, but it was hard to do, even though Troy's words were exactly what he wanted to hear. After being told during one supposed loving relationship that his proclivities were disgusting, it was hard to believe otherwise. He knew now that wasn't the case—the loving part was false in hindsight—but he couldn't shake the words that person threw at him at the time. He had never shown his wants in full colour before the previous night, and it knocked him sideways.

What should he do? Should he leave, cancel the event and avoid Troy in the future? Should he leave but carry on as if it had never happened? Should he stay and hope?

He wanted the last one, but he wasn't sure he could let himself go like that. Words were easily said, but actions were needed to back them up. Decision made, he squeezed Troy's hand and swung his legs over the edge of the bed. Sitting upright, he could see where he'd thrown his clothes and, ignoring his nudity, left the warmth of the bed to retrieve them.

"Don't you want a shower?"

Liam froze for a second and then continued. "I'll grab one at home before work." It was a Bank Holiday, but Troy wasn't to know he didn't work them.

He didn't want to face Troy, but once he was dressed, he could hardly leave without saying something to the man who had made him feel so...real.

He scratched his head and turned, staring at Troy, who looked so fucking sexy sitting in bed with the covers bunched at his waist and with a foot sticking out. His hair was mussed, his cheek had lines from where he'd been sleeping and his chest... He met Troy's gaze.

"Thank you. I...enjoyed myself. A lot. But I need to go."

Troy nodded slowly. "Okay, but can I ask one thing?"

Liam tilted his head. He wasn't sure he could give whatever Troy wanted. "What?" he whispered.

"Can I kiss you goodbye?"

Liam's heart answered, but his voice couldn't. It was the wrong thing to do, but Liam wanted it just as much as Troy seemed to. He stepped closer to the bed without realising he had, and when his knees met the mattress, Troy rose to his knees, the covers falling away as he scooted across the space. The moment he was within arm's reach, Troy slid his hands up Liam's now-covered chest and to his neck. Cupping his nape, Troy pulled him down to meet his mouth. Liam's eyes closed of their own volition, and his hands found Troy's naked hips as Troy slipped his tongue inside Liam's mouth.

A groan escaped his mouth, and Troy deepened the kiss further. Liam's head spun. He needed air, but he needed Troy just as much. When Troy softened the kiss, pulling back, Liam chased his mouth. Troy chuckled and kissed him again softly before setting him back. Liam opened his eyes with effort, and Troy brushed his thumb over Liam's cheeks.

"I'll see you on Saturday?" Troy asked.

Liam swallowed the lump in his throat and nodded, his brain having decided without his input. "Yes," he murmured.

"Good. If you need me before then, call me. Okay?"

Liam closed his eyes and grimaced, wanting it more than he wanted to want it. "Okay," he said when he opened his eyes again.

Troy dropped another kiss on his lips, and Liam stepped back. He spun around so he couldn't see Troy as he exited the room, closing the door behind him. He had a momentary worry that he wouldn't know how to navigate the house, but he saw the stairs and descended without running. He hadn't brought a coat or anything else with him, so he opened the front door, hesitating before leaving.

The closing of the door was like cutting off part of himself, and he had to force himself to do it. By the time he climbed into his car, his heart raced, and he rolled his eyes at himself.

"For fuck's sake, Liam. You're a grown man. Grow some balls."

He started the car and reversed out of the driveway without looking back at the house. And as the miles increased between them, Liam clenched his hands and jaw to prevent himself from turning around. He'd lost himself to someone before, and they had almost ruined him for anyone else. They still might have, but Liam refused to think about that. He also refused to believe that he was capable of love and being loved. If he gave in to that, he would have to push aside everything he wanted for himself. And he wasn't giving up. Not yet.

· · • • ● • ● • • ·

Five days later, he sat in his car, gathering the courage to walk into The Den. He hadn't planned to attend the first mosh pit taster session, but after the week he'd experienced, he needed to let go. And what better way than to show potential pups and handlers what to expect? He was certain Troy wouldn't be there because he had said he wasn't planning to attend. It would give him a couple of hours of relaxing before having to see him for their second practice run. Not that they needed anymore as far as Liam was concerned.

A knock on his window made him jump, so intent on the door to The Den as he'd been, he hadn't seen someone approach. When he stared into the blue eyes he could probably map as well as his own, his heart set off again, competing against the best horse racers in the business.

He scratched his head and pulled his keys from the ignition before opening the door and climbing out to stand beside Troy.

"Hey. I wasn't expecting to see you until later," Troy said.

"Yeah, I've had...a week. I thought I could chill a bit."

"I'm glad I got here when I did then." Troy's gaze dropped to Liam's T-shirt. "*My fashion philosophy is if you're not covered in dog hair, your life is empty. I love it.*" Troy licked his lips. "Are you ever going to get a dog?"

The question came out of nowhere, but Liam nodded. "Eventually."

"Are you not wearing your suit today?"

"I was leaving it for when we met later. I might not even play now, but I needed the..." Liam couldn't think of the words he needed, but Troy answered for him.

"The reassurance of the club?"

"Yeah."

Troy brought his hand up to Liam's cheek slowly. "I wish you would've called me. I might've been able to help," he murmured.

Liam had almost called several times a day, but each time, he forced himself to put the phone down again. He didn't want to seem needy. "It was a busy week."

"Even more reason. But I understand." Troy smiled and removed his hand, though Liam wished it had stayed. "Shall we go in? I'd like to buy you a drink."

They wandered towards the door, and Liam said, "Isn't it my turn?"

"No. I offered."

Liam chuckled. "I can buy drinks, you know."

"I know." Troy held the door open for him when the bouncer nodded at them to enter. "Are we heading straight upstairs, or do you want to relax down here first?"

It wasn't busy in the club, and as much as he wanted to go to the mosh pit area, he also wanted to spend more time with Troy. If Liam saw the mosh pit, he'd probably sink into pup space quicker than ever.

"Down here is fine."

Troy placed a hand on Liam's lower back and led him to the bar. They settled onto two stools, and the bartender took their order. Troy turned his body so his legs were bracketing Liam's body.

"So... You've had a week, you said?"

Liam nodded. He wasn't going to admit that half of it was because he was distracted because of Troy. Instead, he said, "A garden I was landscaping had pipes leading to a supposed defunct water fountain. Those pipes weren't as shut off as I was led to believe. The garden flooded, which meant a big job got a hell of a lot bigger. I had to call in help."

"I hope the clients are footing the bill for that," Troy said, his body tense.

Liam chuckled. "They certainly are. Especially when they admitted afterwards to have known."

"What? That's atrocious."

Liam shrugged. "It is, but they've received a swamp for their lies."

Troy laughed, his hand curling around his glass when the bartender placed it in front of him. "Is it an easy fix? I know we've had problems selling properties when something like that has gone wrong, but we hand it over to people like you to fix."

Liam blew out a breath. "It's not easy, put it that way. It takes time to drain the water, block off the pipes, and then dry out the soil enough to make it a viable garden again. A job that should've taken me a week is going to take another week at least. But I have clients booked for next week, so they're going to have to wait. I'm just glad the weather is warming up nicely."

"Do you get much work in the winter?"

Sipping his lemonade, Liam nodded as he swallowed. "It just changes what things I do. It's not impossible to do a garden on dry days, but I stick to laying slabs, creating patio gardens, that kind of thing."

Troy nodded. "Makes sense."

"Does the weather make a difference in selling houses?" he asked, wanting to palm his forehead at the stupid question.

"Actually, yes." Troy chuckled. "It's much easier to sell a house on a sunny day than it is to sell on a rainy day."

"Seriously?" Liam covered his mouth with his hand, hiding his smile.

Troy nodded. "I've always assumed it's the ambience of a place. If the sun is shining through the windows, it makes everything look ten times better. The same as when you wake up in the morning and sunshine is filtering through the curtains. It perks you up immediately, doesn't it?"

Liam's mind went back to Troy's house and that he had never seen the sun shining through the windows of his balcony. It was a shame because he imagined the sight would be amazing.

"It does. I love being outdoors, anyway."

"You'd have to for your job."

Liam smiled and glanced around them, jumping when a voice started talking by his ear.

"Gentlemen, are you coming up to see the taster session?"

Liam exhaled at Elton's voice and faced him. "Yes. Just having a drink first."

"Good to hear it." He clapped him on his back, Troy receiving the same treatment. "We need couples like you to show them what it's like."

"You have volunteers, don't you?" Liam asked.

Elton nodded. "It never hurts to have more." He winked and wandered off towards the stairs. How the man could walk with such a light step when he was as muscular and tall as he was had always been a mystery to Liam. He'd got to know Elton better after the incident with Vincent, and Robert and Henry had escorted him to Elton's office. Elton had taken care of him after that and made sure he got medical treatment. They weren't best friends or anything, but friends, at least. Elton truly cared about the people in his club.

"I've always wondered how he came to own this place," Troy said.

"I don't know, but it's never been in better hands, in my opinion."

"I agree." Troy grabbed his drink. "Shall we ascend?" He grinned.

Liam snorted. "Ascend?" He stood, holding his drink.

"I'm not wrong."

"It sounds like something from a Jane Austen novel."

"Or maybe *Pirates of the Caribbean.*"

Liam laughed, holding his stomach and steadying his drink with the other hand. "I suppose it could. Do you watch many films?" he asked as they "ascended" the stairs.

"I love watching films. Not so much fun on your own, though."

Liam could hear the inevitable offer Troy would make, and his stomach swirled in anticipation. He doubted he could deny that man anything.

"Do you want to drop straight into pup space, or are you going to watch first?" Troy asked as they found a seat around the mosh pit, which was busier than Liam had ever seen it.

"Let's watch for a bit first. I want to get a feel for those that are here."

Dodo was there with his handler, and he made a beeline for Liam when he saw him. Liam chuckled, scratching behind Dodo's ear.

"I'll be there in a bit, Dodo. Do you want me to throw a ball?" Dodo barked and spun in a circle. Liam reached for the ball Troy held out to him, and Dodo's chest went to the floor, his tail wagging. "Fetch!" He threw the ball to the other side of the pit, towards the other pups as well, and Dodo shot off. Liam wanted to go with him, especially as fetch was his favourite game as a pup.

"You'd be good as a handler, too," Troy said.

Liam shook his head. "I don't mind looking after pups if I need to, but I prefer being one of them." He gulped his drink, finding his mind slowing and heading towards where he wanted to be. He glanced at Troy, who was already looking at him. "Do you want to practise now or later?"

Troy stared at him for a second. "Both."

Liam gazed back at him and nodded slowly. "Okay," he whispered. He slipped off the sofa to the floor, kneeling in front of Troy.

"Present," Troy said.

Liam did, the sounds around them falling away as he closed his eyes. Master's hand petted his head, and Barney moved into it, a whine leaving his mouth.

"Good boy, Barney," Master murmured. "Fetch, boy!"

Barney's head snapped to the side as a ball went bouncing past him. He chased after it, barrelling through a couple of pups along the way. He caught the ball and turned, finding Troy standing near another pup.

"Heel, Barney," Master said.

Barney sat beside Master, batting the ball back and forth while Master spoke to another pup.

"Are you hurt?"

"No, sir. I was just surprised. I didn't move out of the way quickly enough."

"Barney is very focused when he's after a ball. He doesn't always look where he's going. I'm sorry about that." Barney whined, nudging Master's arm. Master glanced at him, a frown on his face.

Barney tilted his head and looked at the other pup, who was rubbing his leg. Barney scooted forward a little, nudging the pup's leg gently and whining again. The pup chuckled.

"It's okay, Barney."

"If you're okay, I'll take him out of the way for a moment."

"He won't be in trouble, will he?" the pup asked.

Master smiled. "Not trouble, no. But he needs a reminder to be careful. He's a very mischievous pup."

The other pup grinned. "I want to be mischievous, too."

"Not too much," Master cautioned. "Only enough to be playful."

"Okay."

Master stood. "Barney, heel." He wandered over to their seats, and Barney settled at his feet. Master leaned forward. "You have to be more careful, Barney. Don't hurt anyone."

Barney glanced at the other pup, who was scooting around the mosh pit with a big smile on his face. He yipped, his muscles bunching to go and play, but he couldn't without Master's say so.

"Wait, Barney. Not yet."

Barney trembled with the need to disobey as he watched the other pups playing.

"Wait..."

Barney whined.

Eight

Troy

Keeping Barney from running off was a battle. Troy could see his body trembling as he kept himself beside Troy, and he pulled a treat from his pocket. Leaning forward again, he petted Barney's head, trying to calm him before letting him play again. Troy was surprised the other pup hadn't been more hurt with how hard Barney had barrelled into him. The other pup had almost flown across the space. Barney whined again, his legs tensing and releasing.

"Good boy, Barney. Here." He held out a treat for him, and Barney yipped and ate it. "Barney." He waited until Barney glanced at him. "Careful. Go play."

Barney barked and bounced off again, stopping just short of the group of pups in the centre of the mosh pit. He bounced forward and retreated, bounced forward and retreated, and then pressed his chest to the floor and wagged his ass, which would usually have had a tail. Another pup moved closer, and they pawed at each other, rolling on the floor as they played, and Troy smiled.

He hadn't expected to meet up with Liam that afternoon, but he was glad he did. Could he persuade Liam to get some dinner before they have another practice run that evening? He didn't want their interactions to only happen at the club, but if that was all he could get, he would take it.

Having not heard from Liam all week was almost more than Troy had been able to bear. Every time he'd opened his phone to find no messages or calls from him, his stomach sank. He didn't think he'd scared him off, but it wasn't an impossibility. Troy could get overbearing sometimes. He didn't think he had, but why else wouldn't Liam have called?

When he'd seen him sitting in his car, Troy couldn't leave it alone. He had to speak to him. It was a visceral need in him. And he'd been rewarded with Liam's presence and, now, with being his handler. How could he show Liam what they could have if they just tried? There was something in Liam's past that had hurt him, Troy could tell, but without him saying the words, all Troy had was guesswork.

He spoke to a couple of people, answering their questions in between looking after Barney, and he finally called Barney to heel an hour and a half later. He didn't want him too exhausted, especially if he insisted on having another practice run that evening, too. Not that Troy thought they needed it. They were certainly compatible.

Barney was reluctant to end their session, but when Troy mentioned dinner, even he heard Barney's stomach growl. Troy petted Barney as he drank, soothing him and bringing him down from the excitement of pup life. When Barney's full weight rested against his legs, he smiled.

"There we go." He brushed his fingers through Liam's hair even as he realised Barney had receded. He didn't want to stop touching him, and while he had an excuse, he would continue.

Liam sighed. "Thank you."

"You're very welcome."

Liam leaned his head back, looking at Troy upside down, and smiled. "I enjoyed that."

"I know you did."

Liam's cheeks darkened. "I'm sorry about hurting that pup. Were they okay?"

Troy nodded. "They were fine. I think you had a lot of energy to burst and weren't paying attention, is all."

"This is what I meant about my behaviour needing to be managed. You did a good job. Every time I did something, I thought about sitting here wanting to play and not being able to. It helped remind me. Or remind Barney."

"Good." Troy continued petting him. "I'd like to take you for dinner before we come back, if that's okay?"

Liam turned his head away, and Troy's stomach fluttered at the move, anticipating the rejection.

"I'd like to cook for you," Liam said, and Troy barely caught it over the noise of the club.

Troy's heart skipped. "Are you sure?"

As if knowing Troy needed to see his eyes, Liam turned to him, resting his chin on Troy's knee. "I'm sure. I make a mean spaghetti carbonara."

Troy chuckled. "Okay."

Liam's eyes lit up. "Really?"

Troy nodded. "If you want to cook, I'm not going to stop you."

Liam stood and held out his hand, helping Troy to stand. "Let's go."

Troy loved the eagerness, and he held Liam's hand as they left the club and headed for Liam's car.

"Do you want me to drive, and I can bring you back to your car later?" Liam asked.

"I'll follow you. That way, we don't have to leave by a certain time."

Troy wasn't planning to spend the night, but he wouldn't deny he wanted to. This way, if they were in the middle of something, they didn't need to fetch his car before the car park locked. Liam texted him his address in case they got separated, but Troy stayed right on his bumper as they drove to Liam's place.

He parked on the street, not being allowed into the car park as it was for residents only, and met Liam by the door to the building. The beep of the door unlocking made Troy feel a little better about the place. Not that it was in a poor area or anything like that, but he had never liked the idea of lots of people living in one building. It was too easy for one of them to let others in, or for them to break into the other apartments in the building itself. But maybe that was his stereotyping getting in the way.

"I don't usually use the lift, but we will this time," Liam said, depressing the button.

"Why not?"

Liam shrugged, fiddling with the keys. "Exercise."

"Don't you get enough of that with your job?"

"Yes, but it never pays to become complacent."

"True."

When the doors enclosed them, Liam held the bar and leaned back, closing his eyes as he rested his head against the wall. Troy took in his white-knuckled hold.

"You don't like lifts, do you?"

Liam opened his eyes, sweat beading on his forehead. His mouth curled on one side. "Not really. Small places in general."

"We could've taken the stairs."

Liam waved him away, gasping when the lift stopped.

As they got off the lift on the fifth floor, Troy realised how much more confident he felt in Liam's presence now. He didn't stumble over his words like he had done to begin with. Was it Liam who helped, or the fact that he was comfortable with him? Or both? He followed Liam down the corridor to the last door, which Liam opened and stepped through. Troy followed, kicking his shoes off just inside.

"This is it," Liam said, gesturing to the open-plan apartment. Troy heard a beep, and Liam sighed. "Sorry, my sister."

Troy frowned. Did his sister live with him? Liam wandered to a small table holding a phone and pressed a button on it.

"Hey, Liam. It's Lora. I've not heard from you for a couple of days. Is everything okay? Yes, I know. I'm being a pain in the ass, but you would, too, if you had a beach ball stuck in your stomach." She sighed. "Anyway, call me back. Love you."

"Lora is your sister?" Troy asked.

"Yes. She's twenty-six."

Troy grinned at the accent that came out when he spoke of his family. Most of the time, he withheld the East End accent, but not always.

Before he could respond, Liam said, "Anyway, dinner."

He moved away, and Troy missed him immediately, even though he was a few feet away at most.

"Feel free to nosey around," Liam said, gesturing to the rest of the apartment. "I've got nothing to hide."

Troy raised his eyebrows, his mouth twitching with the need to smile. "Oh, really?"

Liam opened his mouth and hesitated. "I might regret saying that, but go for it."

As Liam pottered around in the kitchen area, Troy wandered around the living room, studying the knick-knacks Liam must've brought back from his travels, the books on his shelves and the ornaments and decorations Troy was sure Liam hadn't bought himself. The place wasn't big, by any means, but it was the epitome of home in the way Troy didn't think his house was.

Music started playing, and Troy glanced over his shoulder to see Liam set his phone on the counter and smile at him.

"I don't have a stereo, so this will have to do."

"It's perfect." Troy forgot his plans to study everything and settled on a stool at the breakfast bar opposite where Liam worked. "Do you like cooking?"

Liam nodded. "I do. I can't always be bothered to, especially after a long day, but I will when I can."

Liam's hands were sure and steady as he made the food for their dinner, and when he threw it all together and plated it, the smell was divine.

"Enjoy," he said when he sat on the stool beside him.

Troy closed his eyes and inhaled. He forked some into his mouth, moaning as the taste hit his tongue.

"This is delicious," he said.

"Thanks. I didn't realise how hungry I was," Liam said, spearing food into his mouth.

They sat in silence as they ate and drank, and Troy couldn't remember the last time he'd had been so content in someone else's company—apart from Jamie, but he didn't count. He could get used to the idea of sharing a home with Liam, sharing the chores, the cooking, the music. Troy licked his lips. That was one thing he had not shared with Liam. Could he? Did Liam know who Troy's sister was? If he did, then Troy couldn't say anything about his music. He couldn't take the risk.

"Have you heard of Gina Robson, the pianist?"

Liam tilted his head, gazing off into space, then shook his head. "The name doesn't ring a bell."

"She has an amazing talent." He wasn't so ignorant that he wouldn't admit it.

"Yeah?" Liam stared at him. "Do you like her music?"

Troy nodded. "It's a little classical for me, but the ability is extraordinary."

"What music do you like?"

"All kinds. Ed Sheeran, Savage Garden, to name two. But plenty more."

Liam smiled. "We have similar tastes."

Once Troy finished his dinner, he turned on the stool, the same way he had done at the club earlier that night, and bracketed Liam in with his legs. Resting an elbow on the counter, he put his cheek against his fist.

"What do you want to do while we let dinner settle and before we go back for our practice?" Troy asked, wanting Liam to take the lead from there.

Liam licked his lips, staring at his empty plate. His chest rose quicker, and he bit his lip. Troy wanted to bite his lip, too, but he remained silent while Liam worked through whatever he was battling against in his head. Troy knew what he wanted. He wanted Liam, and as much as it scared him to think it, he was falling for him. He hadn't wanted to, not after all the other pups who had let him down, but how could he not fall in love with someone as gentle and kind as Liam?

Liam's phone rang, breaking the silence, and Troy inwardly cursed. Liam cleared his throat and put it on speaker.

"Hey, Paul. How're things?"

"Hey, Uncle Liam! You're going to have a niece or nephew!"

Liam gasped. "She's in labour?"

"Yes, finally," Paul groaned. There was a noise on the other end of the line before Paul said, "Yes, I know. Everything is ready and in the car. I'm just telling Liam. Sorry, she's panicking that we've not got everything ready when we've been ready for weeks. Anyway, we have to go. Are you meeting us at the hospital?"

"Yes! I'm coming."

"Chin up, Uncle Liam. We'll soon be another family member stronger."

Liam braced himself on the counter, and Troy rubbed his hand over Liam's spine.

"Congratulations," he said, leaning down to see Liam's face.

Liam lifted his head, wet eyes meeting his gaze along with a tremulous smile. "I'm going to have a niece or nephew."

Troy smiled. "You will. You don't know their gender?"

Liam wiped his eyes and shook his head. "They won't tell me. It's a surprise, they said." He chuckled. "Lora will be pleased. She's a week overdue and complains bitterly about it, as you heard earlier."

"Now just expect complaints about lack of sleep," Troy joked.

Liam blew out a breath. "Sorry. I wasn't expecting that. I need to..."

"Of course." Troy hesitated and said, "Would you like me to drive? That way you can concentrate."

Liam sniffed. "Are you sure?"

"Positive. Do you need to take anything?"

"Just me, I think. I have gifts, but I don't want to overwhelm them. I'll give them to them another day."

"Let's go, then."

Troy led Liam down the stairs, out of the building and to Troy's car, then aimed for the hospital. They were silent for the first part of the journey until Troy couldn't keep his questions back.

"Where are your parents?"

Liam sighed. "They died eight years ago."

Troy reached over to hold Liam's hand. "I'm sorry."

"It's okay. I spent a few years looking after Lora until she kicked me out."

Troy jerked back, glancing at Liam quickly before returning to the road. "She what?"

Liam chuckled. "Sorry, that came out wrong. I meant she told me to leave and stop hovering over her. She was more than capable of looking after herself, but I didn't want to let her. At least until she told me I needed to find myself." He shrugged. "I left and travelled around the country for a while until I found myself back home again."

"Did you find yourself?"

Liam stared at him. "I'm beginning to."

Troy wanted to read more into that sentence, but he refused to put words into Liam's mouth. Instead, he said, "So it was just you and Lora?"

Liam nodded. "We had no aunts or uncles, no cousins. We're the last of our line."

"Not anymore."

Liam grinned. "I wonder how long the labour will take."

"First babies take longer, so I'm told."

"We could be here for hours, then. You don't have to stay."

Troy shook his head. "I don't mind at all. I can be the one who does drink and snack runs while you concentrate on being an uncle."

"God, Uncle Liam. It's a crazy thought."

"Why?"

"I never expected Lora to want kids. She'd always been vocal about it. Even when she met Paul, I was sure she wouldn't change her mind. At least until she came to me and told me she was pregnant. I had to sit down." He chuckled. "I love the idea of big families who have lots of people to rely on and help and share with."

"Is that what you want?" Troy couldn't help but ask. He felt Liam staring at him, but he didn't take his gaze from the road.

"It is."

Troy smiled. "Make sure you stick with that dream. Don't change it for anyone."

They lapsed into silence again until they reached the hospital, and Troy followed Liam into the maze of corridors and wards. Eventually, they reached their destination when Liam raced down the hallway and into a man's arms. Troy hoped it was his brother-in-law.

"How is she?"

"She's fine. She's just having an epidural and told me to leave so I didn't faint at the needle." Paul's gaze landed on Troy and jerked back to Liam with raised eyebrows.

Liam's cheeks heated as he closed his eyes and winced. If he hadn't been getting to know Liam, he would've taken the expression as something akin to regret, but he'd seen Liam do that whenever he was embarrassed.

"Paul, this is my...friend, Troy. Troy, my brother-in-law, Paul."

Troy held out his hand, and they shook. "Nice to meet you. And congratulations."

Paul grinned. "Thanks."

A nurse opened the hospital room door. "You can come back in now."

Paul stepped closer. "Can her brother see her quickly?"

The nurse smiled and nodded. "Not for long, though. I don't want her overwhelmed."

Troy stayed back as Liam stepped into the room, but Liam popped his head out again. "Do you want to meet my sister?"

Troy raised his eyebrows. "Are you sure?"

Liam grinned. "Definitely."

Troy tried not to read anything into it, but his heart couldn't help the rapid tattoo it made as he stepped in to meet Liam's beloved sister. She was a small, redheaded woman covered by the pristine white covers synonymous with hospitals. Liam leaned over her and kissed her cheek, squeezing her hand as tears fell unchecked down his cheek. Troy loved he was so unashamed of his emotions. All men should be the same, in his opinion.

Lora glanced over at him, and Troy stood straighter. She beckoned him over.

"Lora, this is my friend, Troy. He drove me here. Troy, my sister, Lora."

"Nice to meet you on such a wonderful occasion," Troy said. "I won't intrude for long."

Lora waved her hand. "Stay as long as you want. Someone needs to keep my husband from fainting and my brother from threatening the nurses."

Troy chuckled. "I'll keep that in mind."

"Please do. I have enough to do." She grinned at him and leaned closer to Liam. "He's a keeper."

Liam closed his eyes and shook his head. "Aren't you supposed to be in labour?" he grouched.

"I am," she replied with a smile. "Pain-free labour. I hope," she tacked on the end.

"You'll both be fine," Liam said. "We're not going anywhere."

It was then Troy saw the lines around Lora's mouth, the tension in her body, the worry transmitting from her eyes as she locked gazes with her brother in a silent conversation. Were they worried the baby wouldn't survive? That Lora wouldn't survive? It made sense if their parents had died that they were worried about mortality. It happened a lot from what Troy had read. Whenever someone was touched by death, their fear of their own mortality increased. And if it was more than once, it continued to increase. Another random fact from his mindless research. It wouldn't help them, though.

Nine

LIAM

Lora had never hidden her fear that she wouldn't survive the birth of her child, especially with the complications she had already had throughout. Liam put it down to their parents' dying, but he was convinced she was wrong. She would be there for every step of her child's life, but his conviction wouldn't help her fear. Nothing would help except her survival. And they had several hours to get through before she would be convinced otherwise.

"Would you like something to drink or eat?" Troy asked them.

"I can't have anything, but thank you," Lora said.

"I wouldn't say no to a coffee," Paul said.

"Liam?" Troy asked when Liam didn't answer.

"I'll come with you."

Troy held out his hand. "No, you stay with your family. I'll fetch them. What would you like?"

"Water or lem—"

"Lemonade," Troy finished with a grin. "I'll be back soon." He smiled at Lora, nodded at Paul and exited the room, closing the door quietly behind him.

Liam hadn't realised he'd been staring at the door until Lora squeezed his hand, bringing his attention back to her. She raised her eyebrows at him.

"So, who's Troy?"

Lora didn't know about his lifestyle, but she knew he had trouble settling down. "He's someone I met, and we're...hanging out."

Lora snorted. "Hanging out? What are you, fourteen?"

"I don't know what else to say. We're friends. There might be more, but not yet. I'm taking it slowly."

His sister sighed. "You need to take the chance, Liam. I want to see you happy."

"I am happy."

She glared at him. "You know what I mean."

Liam clenched his jaw. He did know what she meant, but it didn't make it any easier to accept that Troy was who he said he was and that Liam was enough for him. He wasn't sure he would ever get over that hill.

A knock sounded, and a nurse bustled in. "Good evening, Lora. Let's have a look at you, shall we?"

"On that note, I'm going to step outside," Liam said, leaning over to kiss his sister's cheek before heading out of the room. Troy was exiting the lift with a tray as he closed the door, and Liam gestured at the seats along the corridor. Troy set the tray on one seat and sat beside Liam.

"Is everything okay?" Troy asked, gesturing to the door.

"Yes. She's just being checked by the nurse. You don't have to wait, you know. It might be hours."

"I don't have any other plans. I'm happy to stay if you'd like me to."

And Liam wanted him to. Not because he didn't want to be alone, but because he wanted Troy with him. He wanted to spend more time with him and share this event with someone other than Lora and Paul.

Taking a breath, he murmured, "I'd like you to stay."

Troy's smile lit up the already bright corridor, and Liam couldn't help but mirror the expression, though he ducked his head as he did.

"Shall we bet how long it will be?" Troy asked.

Liam chuckled. "Okay. I say twelve hours."

Troy tapped his chin, staring at the ceiling. "I say seven hours."

"You'll be lucky if it's that quick. Or should I say, Lora will be lucky if it's that quick."

"You never know."

Liam settled back and opened his bottle of lemonade, taking a sip of the tart, fizzy liquid and sighing as he finished. "That hits the spot."

"Glad to hear it." Troy sipped his drink and then said, "I know we didn't get to practise again tonight, but I don't think we need one, do you?"

Liam cocked his head, thinking about his words. They were compatible, without a doubt, and he hoped they would do all right in front of the attendees at the festival. "I think we'll be fine. Are you still nervous about being in front of so many people?"

Troy waved his hand back and forth. "I'm still a little unsure, but I think it's mainly because I don't know what to expect. Although I've attended a Pride festival before, I've never been involved in one. I don't want to mess up. The actual task of being your handler is not a problem for me." He smiled, and Liam studied his features. His blue eyes were so expressive, and his dark blond hair seemed untameable. But it was the slight lines around his eyes that showed how much he smiled, and how at ease he was with the situation.

"You won't mess up. Just forget about the people around you and focus on me."

"That's no hardship," Troy said, bumping his shoulder against Liam's, making Liam laugh.

The door to Lora's room opened, and the nurse came out with a smile for them. "We're all done."

Troy picked up the tray, and Liam held the door open for him to enter. Paul took his coffee with a glare from his wife, and Lora gestured for him to move.

"Troy, come sit with me and tell me all about you. I need the distraction."

The nurse came in several times over the course of the next five hours, and everyone was looking exhausted. Lora had told them to leave and come back in the morning, but Liam had refused, with Troy echoing the sentiment. Troy had made several more trips for drinks and food, and after the last nurse's visit, they had good news.

"You're almost there, Lora. You'll be bringing this beauty into the world soon."

Lora exhaled. "I'm glad. I'm a little bored with waiting now."

The nurse laughed. "That's the burden of an epidural. No pain, but you are bored because you have nothing to concentrate on except for your guests."

Troy winked at Liam. "I guess I win."

Liam scrunched his forehead before he realised he spoke about their bet. "She's not given birth yet. Don't count your chickens."

As Troy laughed, Liam got lost in his thoughts. There was more to Troy than met the eye, and although he had answered almost all of Lora's questions, there were some he had avoided, changing the subject or throwing the question back on Lora herself. It was a neat trick that Liam would have to learn, but it raised his interest. Why didn't Troy tell them about his family, other than to say he had parents and a sister? He didn't say much about where he grew up, but he spoke in great detail about music and films and houses. Liam could tell what he was passionate about, including being a handler, though that never came up.

It took another three hours, but Lora was finally given the green light to bring her baby into the world. Liam and Troy left the room, allowing the new parents to experience it alone, and settled into the uncomfortable chairs outside. They didn't say much, but Troy slid his arm around Liam's shoulders, allowing Liam to rest his head on Troy's shoulder and close his eyes. He didn't sleep or doze, but he enjoyed their closeness.

When they finally heard the cry of a baby, Liam's head shot up, nearly clipping Troy's chin. A smile spread across his face as he waited, but it was another half an hour before a nurse opened the door to gesture them inside.

Lora was sweat-soaked, rosy-cheeked and smiling as she stared down at the bundle in her arms. Paul had his arm around his wife and was also looking down. Liam stepped closer, and Lora glanced up.

"Hey, Uncle Liam. Would you like to meet Lula?"

"Lula?" he whispered. "She's a girl?" Lora nodded, and Liam felt a hand at his back, gently nudging him forward. He leaned closer, smiling at the pink bundle wrapped in a white blanket. "Hello, Lula. Welcome to the family."

His heart burst with love for the little human, and he met his sister's gaze with tears in his eyes. "Was everything okay?"

Lora glanced at Paul and back again. "I lost too much blood, but they were prepared. It could've been worse, but these guys are amazing." She gestured to the nurses and doctor that were finishing up. "We're good."

"I won't say I told you so," he joked, pressing his lips to Lora's temple.

"Congratulations to you both," Troy said.

Liam rose, peering at the man who hadn't needed to stay but did, anyway. "Thank you for being here. I'm glad you could share this with us," he murmured.

"I'm glad I could be here. This is..." Troy choked up and didn't finish, but Liam thought he understood the gist of it.

They spent a short time with the new parents and baby Lula before they said their goodbyes and closed the door on the new family. Liam leaned against the wall and rested his head back, blowing out a long breath.

"Are you okay?" Troy stepped right up to him, and Liam lifted his head.

"That was intense."

Troy nodded. "You need to sleep."

"So do you." Liam inhaled and listened to his heart for once. "Come home with me?" he whispered. "To sleep. That's all."

Troy's smile was beautiful. "I'd love to."

No other words were said after Troy threaded their fingers together and led Liam out of the hospital and back to the car. Troy declined the offer to pay for parking—which wasn't cheap because they'd been there so long—and soon they were on their way back to Liam's house.

The remnants of the dinner they'd shared so many hours before were still on the table, and Liam cleared it away into the kitchen for him to deal with the following day. Then he had nothing else to do, and he stared at Troy as if waiting for instructions, even though it was his house.

Troy seemed to understand and stepped closer. "It's time for bed, Liam. Show me where your bedroom is."

Liam nodded, eyes feeling heavier already, and led the way to his bedroom. It wasn't as tidy as it should have been, but he'd rarely had any visitors other than Lora, Paul and Val. He dragged some clothes off the bed and onto a chair in the corner of the room. Facing Troy, he lifted his hands to his T-shirt hem.

"Wait," Troy said. He came forward and removed Liam's hands, replacing them with his own. He tugged the T-shirt over Liam's head, unfastened his jeans and pushed them down, leaving him in his briefs. He led Liam over to the bed, pulling the covers back. "Get in."

Liam did but rolled to his side so he could watch Troy undress. He wasn't disappointed, except to say that there was no way he could do anything about his need for the man because of how tired he was. When Troy slid into the bed, Liam rolled to his other side and snuggled into Troy's arms, resting his head on his chest. The warmth of him and the steady beat of his heart lulled Liam to sleep before he could say anything else to Troy.

His phone woke him, ringing somewhere in the room, and he groggily sat upright, trying to open his eyes enough to search the room. His gaze lingered on Troy for a few seconds, who was also trying to rouse, and then he climbed out of bed to grab his discarded jeans. The phone went silent before he could pull it free, and when he saw the screen, he groaned and fell back onto the bed, closing his eyes again. He jumped when the phone rang in his hand. He swiped at it and held it to his ear.

"What?"

"Morning. Are you still coming today?" Robert asked.

"Coming where?" Liam murmured.

"At Book Drunk. There's a small celebration for Kieren's birthday, remember? We'd made plans."

At that, Liam rubbed his eyes and sighed. "Shit. I forgot, Robert. Lora had her baby."

"She did!" Robert made excited noises on the other end of the line. "That's fantastic. Boy or girl? What did they call them? Was it before or after midnight? Because if they share a birthday with Kieren, that would be awesome."

Liam snorted and sat upright, knowing he wouldn't sleep any more. Robert was a lot more into children than he'd expected when they'd first met. "She's a girl called Lula, and it was after midnight, so she does, in fact, share a birthday with Prince Kieren."

"He's not a prince yet, you know," Robert said.

"Regardless. He may as well be."

"True. Can't ever see them splitting up." Robert paused. "I'll let them know you can't make it. Give our love to Lora and her family."

Liam glanced at Troy, who was staring at him with a crease between his eyebrows. "You know what? I'll be there. Is it okay to bring a guest?"

"Of course."

"All right. I'll see you in half an hour or so."

"Sure thing. We'll be here most of the day. We've shut the cafe to the public and blocked out all the windows so we have privacy."

"It would've been easier to do it at the castle, you know."

"Don't I know it," Robert groused. "But Patrick wanted it here."

"Fair enough. See you soon."

He ended the call and said, "Do you fancy going to a birthday party?"

Troy raised his eyebrows, and Liam could see him connecting the dots. "You want me to go to a prince's birthday party?"

Liam grinned. "They're not so high and mighty that they aren't friends with other people, you know. Most of the princes' partners are commoners."

"Yes, but still." Troy rubbed his head. "I think this is more terrifying than the idea of being in front of thousands of people at the festival."

Liam chuckled and stood. "You'll be fine. I'm going for a shower, then you can have at it."

He took the quickest shower known to man and dried himself quickly. Troy jumped in when Liam exited, and Liam pulled on some fresh jeans and a T-shirt that said, "*I feel sorry for people who don't have dogs. I hear they have to pick up food they drop on the floor.*" Then he pulled a black shirt over the top, leaving the buttons unfastened for now. After a few minutes of deliberation, he pulled out another pair of jeans and a shirt for Troy. He had no idea if they would fit him, but they could always go to Troy's house if they didn't.

When Troy emerged with a towel wrapped around his waist, Liam lost his voice. He held out the clothes without a word, and Troy smiled and took them.

"Do you—" Liam's voice squeaked, and he cleared his throat, trying again. "Do you need underwear as well? I don't know if any of it will fit."

"Only if you don't mind me using them. Jeans chafe a little when I don't wear anything underneath."

Liam pulled a pair of boxers free. They were ones he rarely wore because he preferred briefs. He couldn't pull his gaze from Troy as he dressed as if Liam wasn't present, not hiding anything from him as he dropped his towel and pulled the boxers up his legs. He stepped into the jeans, pulled the shirt on, then fastened everything and ran his fingers through his hair.

"Will I do?"

Liam blinked, trying to understand the words. "Um, yeah. Sorry."

Troy stopped in front of Liam, sliding his hands up Liam's chest. "Don't be sorry for looking at me, Liam." He cupped Liam's nape and dropped a kiss on his lips. "Shall we go?"

Liam nodded.

"Is there anything I need to know before we get there?" Troy asked as they drove to the town centre.

"I don't think so. They're all pretty down to earth. Even with everything that's been going on."

"I feel like I'm gatecrashing," Troy said, chuckling.

Liam smiled. "You'll be fine. This will be nothing compared to the wedding I attended."

"What wedding?" Troy asked, eyes wide.

"I went to Prince Henry's wedding a few weeks ago."

"No shit!" Liam laughed, holding his stomach as Troy's surprised outburst echoed around the car. Troy parked and scooted around to face him. "Seriously?"

Liam nodded, regaining his breath. "They're my friends. How else did you think I got an invite?"

Troy exhaled. "Wow. That's amazing."

Liam opened his car door. "Come on. I'm late as it is."

They headed down the street towards the cafe book shop he always visits with his sister and knocked on the door. A face appeared when the window covering was moved, and then the door opened, and they slipped inside. The cafe looked the same except for the decorations hanging from every conceivable place, all dangling down enough to strangle someone if they were caught unawares.

"Liam! Glad you could make it."

Prince Henry held out his hand, and they shook. "Thanks for inviting me. I still can't get used to being friends with a prince."

Henry laughed. "As we always keep telling you, we don't bite. And we welcome newcomers." His gaze slid to Troy, and Troy introduced himself.

"Troy Gibson, nice to meet you, Your Highness," he said, head bowing.

Henry shook his hand. "Please, none of that today. You'd be doing it all day if you did. Let me introduce you to everyone."

Liam saw the wide-eyed expression on Troy's face and laughed. Maybe he wasn't the only one feeling overwhelmed.

Ten

Troy

Meeting the members of the royal family had never been on his radar. Ever. Although he lived in the same town as them and had seen them in passing, he had never expected to properly meet and be introduced to them. It was...a lot. But Prince Henry—just Henry—was pulling him around the room to meet the princes and princes-to-be. He'd met all but two when his name was called.

"Troy Robson, I'll be damned." Prince Patrick came right up to him and shook his hand. "Gina's brother, right?"

It was then everything clicked, and his chest got tight. He hadn't wanted that part of his world to touch this part, but it was inevitable, he supposed. He'd forgotten that Patrick was a piano player and an amazingly talented one at that. Of course, he would've known about Gina. Few people in the music industry didn't.

"Yeah, I am."

"How are you? I didn't realise you were still around these parts. I know Gina has moved on, hasn't she?"

Troy swallowed past the lump in his throat. "She has. She is in Australia with our parents at the moment, halfway through the world tour."

"Exciting stuff. Do you not want to go with her?" Patrick asked.

Troy shook his head. "She's the talented one of the family. I'm happy here."

"I'm sure you have plenty of talents, Troy. It's great to see you. I'm sorry we haven't met before now, but I'm glad you could be here. Let me introduce the birthday boy."

Troy tried to concentrate on what they were saying as he was introduced to Kieren, but his mind was on Liam, who had been giving him strange looks during the conversation. There was bound to be some backlash for not telling Liam who he was. Granted, he had mentioned Gina, asking Liam if he'd known who she was, but he hadn't offered the information about his relation to her. He hadn't thought it mattered. How wrong could he be?

They settled at a table with a drink and some cake as people mingled, and Liam stared at him. "Why did you ask if I knew Gina?"

Troy exhaled, moving the remains of his cake around his plate with the fork. He put it down and linked his fingers, staring down at them. "To cut a long story short, and I'm not saying this for any kind of sympathy, when my parents realised how much talent Gina had, they pushed her to be the best. I don't begrudge her at all. But they practically forgot who I was. I did not purchase the house I live in, and it's not a house I would've chosen for myself. My parents insisted I had something worthy of their name. I don't announce who I'm related to because I'm nothing like them. At least, I hope I'm not."

Liam's hands covered his. "Just from the little you've told me, you're nothing like them. You're kind, helpful, friendly, and that makes you a thousand times more worthy in my eyes."

Troy swallowed hard, meeting Liam's gaze and seeing the truth in his eyes.

"Is that why you don't play any instruments?"

Troy lowered his eyes, not wanting to lie, but unsure about being truthful.

"Ah." Troy met Liam's gaze again. "You do play, but no one knows." Liam tilted his head. "I won't pry, but know that I would love to hear you play, even if you can't carry a tune."

Troy laughed and turned his hands over to capture Liam's in his, squeezing in thanks. "I never wanted anyone to use my talent against me, so I've only ever told one person. My music teacher."

Liam's eyebrows raised. "How did you keep that quiet?"

Troy smiled at the memory of the conversation he'd had with Mr Royce.

"Mr Royce?" Troy said hesitantly.
"Yes, Troy?"

Now he was here, he wasn't sure exactly what to say to explain. But he had to try. "I want to learn to play the flute."

"That's wonderful! I can give you a letter to take home to your parents—"

"No!" Troy held out his hand to stop him. He licked his lips. "They can't know."

Mr Royce settled into his seat and frowned at him. "Why not? They'd be excited to know they had a second talented musician in the family, would they not?"

That was exactly why he didn't want them to know. "They would, but..."

When Troy didn't finish, Mr Royce continued to stare at him before his expression cleared, as if a light bulb had lit. "You don't want to go on stage?"

"Not as a puppet for them," Troy spat.

Mr Royce raised his eyebrows. "You're a little young to be so sure about what you want."

Troy stood straighter. "All my life, I've seen how they treat Gina, experienced how they treat me. I'd much prefer to be in my shoes, regardless of how much money I could make."

His teacher smiled at him. "We have a quandary then."

"Why?"

"Because unless your parents agree, we cannot offer you lessons with this teacher."

Troy's shoulders fell, his head bowing as his chance withered away in front of him.

"But maybe I can help."

Troy's gaze snapped up to his. "How?"

Mr Royce pulled a box from underneath his desk, opened it and fiddled with something Troy couldn't see. Then he *lifted the sparkling silver flute to his mouth and played a song Troy would forever remember.*

"I think I can help," Mr Royce said. "And no one has to know."

When Troy finished telling his story, Liam had a smile on his face, and Troy felt lighter. He hadn't realised the weight of his secret until some of it eased.

"I'd love for you to play for me."

Troy nodded slowly. "One day."

"Promise?" Liam's eyes sparkled.

Troy shook his head, his mouth twitching. "There's that mischievous spirit again. I promise." He looked away for a second, then met Liam's gaze again. "I'm sorry I didn't tell you."

Liam waved him away. "You didn't need to. We're only..." he trailed off.

"We're only what?" Troy murmured, locking Liam to him with his eyes. When he didn't finish his sentence, Troy said, "Because from where I'm sitting, we're not *only* anything. This is..." He waved his hand between them and gathered his thoughts. "This is more than expected, but I refuse to let the chance pass me by."

"The chance of what?" Liam whispered.

"You know what." Liam's face froze, and Troy understood it was too much to think about right then, so he changed the subject. "So, how did you become friends with a prince?"

Liam sipped his drink. "Um, I can say I was in trouble and they helped, but the rest is not my story to tell," he said, just as Robert stopped by their table.

"Whose story?" Robert asked.

Liam chuckled. "Yours. Troy was asking how we met."

Robert waved him away. "I'm a handler and Henry is my pup. We played at The Den a few times, and when Liam got into trouble, we helped him out of it. But not before that asshole did a number on your ribs. I'm still pissed about that."

"You're not the only one," Liam said. "So, yeah. That's how we met." He turned to Robert. "I wasn't sure how open you were being. And I think someone wants you." He pointed behind Robert.

"Between friends, we're good. Everyone knows everything by this point, I think." Robert glanced over his shoulder to where Henry was waving at him. "I'll see you later."

And so the day went on, conversations with princes and princes-to-be about weddings, birthdays, parties, relationships, and every other imaginable topic was covered, and by the end, Troy was exhausted. But in a good way. He got to spend time with Robert and Henry and watch the banter between them and Liam. He found out things about the royals he never thought he'd know and would take to his grave. It wasn't until Patrick brought out his instruments that he felt uncomfortable in any way.

The prince started with the clarinet, a mysterious fun tune that had everyone clapping along. Troy smiled at the antics, glad Liam had introduced him to them. Next, Patrick brought out his violin, a soulful melody floating through the air that had Troy's eyes closing as the notes sank into him. Then he set up his flute, and Troy stiffened to stop himself from reacting. But as the beautiful tones of a classical song played through the room, he found his fingers twitching along with the notes. He wanted to join in but couldn't.

"Go and play," Liam whispered in his ear. Troy shook his head. "They would love to hear you, and they wouldn't make you do anything you didn't want to."

"I don't know if I can."

At that moment, he glanced back at Patrick and saw the man staring at him as he finished the song. Everyone clapped, and Patrick thanked them, then headed over to where Liam and Troy sat. Patrick crouched beside him.

"You play the flute, don't you? I saw your fingers moving as I played."

Troy couldn't answer. His stomach was in knots. All he could see was his future laid out before him with rehearsal after rehearsal, concert after concert, practice after practice, and he hated it.

Patrick tilted his head. "I don't want to push you because I can see something is worrying you. But if you want to play..." He laid the flute on the table in front of Troy, then squeezed Troy's shoulder as he moved away.

Troy stared at the instrument, a need rising in him to hold it, to play it as it always did whenever he was close to his instrument of choice. He scrunched his face and stared at the floor instead of where he wanted to look. He wasn't a prodigy in any way, shape or form, but he wasn't bad either. Would someone try to force him to play in the spotlight? Would someone tell his parents? His sister?

For the first time in a long time, he wanted to show someone what he could do, but he didn't want to share it with his family. He wanted this moment just for them. Was he willing to take the chance that no one would find out?

He licked his lips and rubbed his forehead, his free hand reaching for the flute of its own accord. His eyes ran along the glossy surface, his fingertips nestling against the smooth keys. Taking a breath, he closed his eyes, put the flute to his lips and played.

Everything around him disappeared as he fell into the first song Mr Royce had ever taught him. The song Mr Royce had played that fateful day. *Fly Me to the Moon.* He lost himself in the music, letting the memories of a time gone by float to the surface. The secret lessons, his small room, the joy he felt when he played, and when he finished the piece, he sighed.

His eyes snapped open at the applause, and his cheeks flushed. Every member of the party clapped and smiled his way, and he carefully put the flute back on the table, his hands trembling.

"That was amazing," Liam said, leaning across the space. Troy stared at him, the moisture in Liam's eyes a telling sign Troy hadn't made a mess of things.

"Thanks."

"When I said you could play, I didn't imagine you were that good," Patrick said after he'd rejoined them. "Who taught you?"

Troy cleared his throat. "My primary school teacher. Nobody knew but us."

"But why? That is talent right there."

With his stomach churning, Troy met Patrick's gaze. "And that is why I tell no one. I don't want to be a monkey performing for the masses. I don't want to be paraded in front of thousands of people just because of what I can do. I want to live my life my way, without interference from people who believe they know better than me." He inhaled and winced. "Sorry, I wasn't implying you were doing that," he added.

Patrick waved him away with a smile. "You weren't, and I understand completely." He tapped his thumbs together. "Is that what they did with Gina?"

Troy wasn't surprised Patrick had picked up on the undercurrent of Troy's anger. He nodded. "I don't know if it was what Gina truly wanted, or if she wanted to do what our parents told her to, but the number of hours she put into everything involved in her career was more than I could take."

"It does take an inordinate amount of time." Patrick crouched beside him. "I want to talk to you about it a little more, though. But not here. I've started offering free music lessons to those children who can't afford to pay for them, and I'd love you to have a look and see if you would consider helping. We need teachers who are willing to donate their time. Because we don't get paid for it." Patrick chuckled.

Troy's initial reaction was to decline, but when he glanced at the flute, he realised he could help so many people, and he didn't have to tell anyone he didn't want to.

"I'd love to know more."

Patrick beamed. "Fantastic! I'll grab your phone number before you leave and we can sort it all out." He stood and held out his hand. "You have great talent, Troy. I would be honoured to have you on board."

Troy shook hands and smiled. "Thanks." He faced Liam, whose smile had spread across his face. "What?"

"Nothing. You just seem...more content."

Troy checked in with himself and realised Liam was right. Having played in front of these people had lifted a weight from his shoulders, and although he had no intention of pursuing a music career, he would happily help those who needed it.

"I'm going to have to channel my inner Mr Royce," he said.

Liam chuckled. "That shouldn't be too hard. He was a significant influence on you, from what I can tell. You probably have him talking inside your head at random points throughout your days, don't you?"

Troy snorted into his drink, almost spitting it all over himself. He wiped his chin. "You'd be right. My parents weren't bothered what I did as long as it shone favourably on the family. Any time I wasn't at home, they assumed I had an after-school club I went to. Whatever paperwork

I put in front of them, they signed with barely a glance. I couldn't take that chance with the music, though. I didn't want to become what Gina has. She seems happy, so I can't say it was a terrible choice for her, but it's not for me. However, teaching others to play music might just be something I could do."

"You'd be great at it if your playing is anything to go by."

"We'll see. Teaching is a lot different from playing."

"You teach pups to be calmer, to follow rules. Surely it's not much different."

Troy's mouth twitched. "Like I'm teaching you to be calmer?"

Liam covered his mouth with his hand, hiding the smile that Troy knew would be there. "Maybe don't use me as an example." He chuckled. "Besides, we've only had a couple of sessions."

"Are you okay with that, or do you want more before next weekend?"

Liam shook his head. "I think we know we're compatible. I doubt we'll have any problems at the festival."

"I'm still a little nervous."

Liam covered his hand with his own. "You don't need to be. Just concentrate on me and pretend there's no one else there."

"Although that is sound advice, if I pretend no one else is there, I could go too far." He winked at Liam, and Liam closed his eyes and bit his lip.

"Yeah, maybe hold back on that." Liam exhaled. "Are you busy tonight?"

"Unfortunately, yes. I have prior arrangements. This week is busy for me at work, too. I could be free on Friday?"

Liam shook his head. "I'm not. Val's coming into town for the weekend to celebrate the festival with me."

"Val?"

"My best friend. He lives in Edinburgh."

Troy nodded, glad he didn't have to compete with someone else for the chance at Liam's heart. "So, next Saturday before the event, then? Can I call you this week, though?"

Liam smiled. "Definitely."

They gazed at each other, their fingers twined as best they could from across the table, and Troy couldn't remember being happier than he was at that moment. Surrounded by royalty, he felt more at home than he ever had. And didn't that say everything about the state of his relationship with his family?

Eleven

LIAM

L iam hadn't believed waiting a week to see Troy would be much of a hardship. How wrong he was. He wanted to speak to him all the time. Tell him about his day. The stories his clients told him as he worked. It was only through sheer force of will that he didn't blow up Troy's phone every minute of the day. He wasn't that type of person. Or so he'd thought.

When had being with Troy become such a necessity for him? To begin with, he had been reticent and unwilling to give himself to anyone, but somehow, Troy had sneaked beneath his defences and lodged himself somewhere in the region of Liam's heart. And that was after only a few weeks.

He refused to count the months he'd been eyeing him at the club.

Liam struggled with the knowledge that he'd let Troy in further than he'd meant to, but he couldn't stop himself from following the road he was now on. He didn't want to. There was something about Troy that drew Liam like a pup after a frisbee. And for the first time in a long time, he found he wanted to follow wherever this relationship went. Even if they hadn't defined anything yet.

When the day of the Windsor Pride Festival dawned, Liam was already awake and raring to go, even after the late night he'd had with Val. He would be exhausted by the end of the day, but if he played his cards right, maybe he could finish the day in someone else's arms. Val would understand if they couldn't hang out all night.

With the weather promising warm temperatures, instead of his usual pup suit, he slid on some black leather trousers that had a cotton liner to help with the potential sweating, a T-shirt—that day's quote was, "*Sorry, I can't. I have plans with my dog*"—and a leather harness that criss-crossed around his chest. He would wear his usual mask, gloves and shoes, but he didn't want to be too hot when he would be in the sunshine during the warmest part of the day.

His phone beeped, and he dived for it, practically jumping over the bed to the table where it was plugged in.

TROY: *Good morning. I have a feeling you're already up. I couldn't sleep. I'm still a little nervous, but I'm trying to keep a cool head. I'm glad I'll have you by my side. x*

Liam couldn't stop the smile from spreading across his face as his fingers raced across the screen.

LIAM: I'll be right there with you. Just focus on me and you'll be fine. Aren't you even a tiny bit excited? x

He wanted to wait for Troy's reply, but he also wanted to finish getting ready so he and Val could get to the festival. They wanted to see some of the other parts of it before Liam had to "perform." He grabbed everything and headed down the hallway without banging on Val's door to wake him up like he used to have to do. Adam must've trained him well in the intervening years because, as he entered the kitchen, the scent of coffee hit him.

"Coffee? I would've thought you'd be drinking tea."

Val snorted into his mug and gulped the liquid as if it was life-affirming fluid—which, to some people, it would be. "I've had four hours of sleep, hotshot. Coffee is the blood running through my veins today."

Liam held up his hand as he sipped the drink waiting for him. "Don't blame me. You're the one who wanted to stay and watch the drag night."

"You have to admit it was amazing." Val raised his eyebrows over his mug, his hazel eyes twinkling at him.

"It was fantastic. That wasn't the issue." Liam chuckled. "Anyway, are you ready?"

Val spread his hands, surprisingly keeping all the liquid inside the mug. "Do I look ready?"

Liam tilted his head and turned, rifling through a kitchen drawer. He threw his gift to Val, the man barely catching the box of matches. "You might need these for your eyelids."

He strode for the front door to the music of Val's curses.

An hour later, those curses were repeated when they got shoved and jostled along with the crowds as they wound their way through the initial streets towards the main event starting point. The atmosphere was electric, but the sheer number of people could be overwhelming. Hopefully, Troy wouldn't get too anxious about the audience size. Liam would have to think of something to distract him.

They chatted over the music, danced along with the strangers beside them and sang at the top of their voices as they worked towards Book Drunk, where Liam had agreed to meet Troy. Excusing themselves as they drew closer, they weaved through the people, and Liam made Troy jump when he popped up beside him.

"Hey," Liam said, unable to stop the grin from spreading across his face.

"Hey, yourself. Are you having a good time?" Troy's smile lit up the day, even though the sun already shone brightly. He was similarly dressed to Liam, with his usual leather trousers and shirt but minus his jacket.

"Definitely. Have you looked around at all?"

Troy shook his head, leaning forward so Liam could hear him. "I kind of got carried along as I aimed for here, then had to swim through the tide before it swept me past this place."

Liam chuckled. Someone elbowed him, and he glanced to the side, finally remembering Val was with him. "Sorry! Troy, this is my best friend, Val. Val, this is Troy, my handler."

Val studied Liam, who squirmed because Val knew him too well, and then focused on Troy. "Nice to meet you, Troy. You've got your hands full with this one."

Troy laughed, though the sound was carried away by the crowds. "And don't I know it."

Val peered at Lim and thumbed towards Troy. "He's got your number."

"Yeah, yeah. All right. I get the picture." He focused on Troy. "Are you ready?"

Troy blew out a breath. "As ready as I'll ever be." His eyes darted towards the people surrounding them.

"You'll be perfect. I know it." Liam smiled when Troy met his gaze and nodded. Liam spoke to Val, though kept his gaze on Troy. "Val, we'll see you in a couple of hours, yeah?"

"Right back here," Val said, clapping his shoulder.

"Shall we?" Liam raised his eyebrows.

Troy held out his hand, and Liam didn't hesitate to link their fingers. He led the way through the crowds, squeezing Troy's hand now and then, until they reached the float they would play on. It was the kind of float that was set on the back of an empty lorry. Whoever had organised it had done a good job. The crowds could see every part of the "play area" because they had fixed clear plastic panels along the base of where they would be. Liam assumed it was to stop anyone from falling off, which was a possibility with how rambunctious the pups could get, but also to stop any balls or equipment from escaping. He could just imagine a handler throwing a ball for a pup and the ball—and pup—flying into the crowd when they both fell off the lorry.

"Liam, Troy. Just who we need," Elton said, waving them over. "We've got ten minutes until we start moving, so get yourselves organised." He pointed to the steps to climb up to the float. "Chop, chop!"

Liam chuckled and saluted. "Yes, sir."

They climbed onto the lorry, which was surprisingly sturdy for being empty, and headed over to the person who was coordinating the float itself.

"Right, everyone's here. I'm Lucy, and I'm the person you need to come to if you need anything. So, this parade will wind its way through the whole of Windsor. It will take around an hour, but you don't need to be on point for the whole of that time. If you need to stop or rest or anything like that, do so without worrying. If you need anything, I'll be right over there." She pointed to the back of the lorry cab, where an armchair sat in the centre. "I am a paramedic, too, so if there are any problems, we should be good. If at any point there is an emergency, there are two red buttons." She pointed at them, one at each end of the lorry. "Press them without fear of recrimination, and the driver will stop immediately. Any questions?"

Liam shook his head, as did everyone else.

"Okay, then. The fundamental rule is to have fun. The only other thing I want to say is that we have some promotional bouncy balls. Feel free to throw them into the crowd if you wish, but it's not essential, as I know you'll be having fun in your relevant roles. We leave in four minutes."

Liam sighed and glanced at Troy. "Are you ready?"

Troy chuckled. "Stop asking me that. My answer will always be the same." He clapped his hands together. "Shall we get into it?"

"Yes, Master." Liam took the collar from his pocket and held it out. "Will you do the honours?"

Troy's Adam's apple bobbed, and then he took the collar. "Present."

Liam dropped to his knees and stared up at his handler, his master, his...lover? Brushing aside the thought to return to later, he closed his eyes when Troy leaned down to fasten the collar Troy had made for him around his neck. As the leather rested against his skin, he breathed in Troy's scent, smiling to himself. No matter what came after this, he would enjoy the event. When Troy pulled away, Liam missed his warmth, but he dutifully opened his eyes and peered up at his master.

"One minute!" Lucy called.

Troy smiled and ran a hand over Liam's hair. "Mask?"

Liam pulled the mask from his back pocket, pulled it over his head, and the quick change from Liam to Barney began. Troy pulled Liam's gloves from his other back pocket and helped him to put them on.

"And we're off!" Lucy shouted. Everyone cheered, Liam and Troy included.

There was a judder as the lorry started on the route over twenty other lorries were following. Hundreds of people were involved, thousands if he included the people who had just come to watch. Each lorry had people dancing, singing, walking in between them, and Liam could see some pups he knew on the ground between their lorry and the next.

"Barney!" Troy called, and Barney's head whipped around, his brain having already dropped enough into pup space that hearing his name had taken him fully down. "Come here, boy!" Master clapped his thighs, and Barney scampered over to him, almost bowling him over. "Oof! Careful, Barney," Master said with a laugh, scratching Barney's ear as he nuzzled his thigh.

Barney heard a yip followed by a bark and turned to the sound. Two pups rolled on the floor, swiping at each other, and Barney raced over to join in. He fell on top of them, yipping, and rolled to the side, nudging them with his nose. He danced out of the way when one swiped at him, then pounced back. A whistle sounded, and several balls bounced past them. Barney wanted a ball, but he wanted to play with these pups, too. His attention was divided, but when the other pups ran for a ball, he joined them. The balls were of different sizes, and Barney nosed a small one, sending it rolling away. When he reached it, he nosed it again, sending it spiralling off across the space.

"Barney!" A short, sharp whistle sounded, and Barney swung his head around. "Food!"

Barney scampered to his master, crashing into him and sending him several steps backwards. Master chuckled. "I'm going to need to brace myself whenever I call you from now on, I think." He shook a bag. "Sit." Barney did, mouth watering as he focused on the bag.

Master held up a shallow metal bowl and poured something into it. Barney wagged his tail with every little clink he heard. When Master finished, he rattled the bowl, and Barney yipped, wanting to jump up but knowing he shouldn't.

"Good boy." Master placed the bowl on the floor, and Barney jumped on it, chomping the treats quickly while Master rubbed his back.

When he finished, he lifted his head, and Master poured some water into the now-empty bowl. Barney lapped at it. Then he heard some noise and tilted his head, looking around him to find the source of the noise. He trotted over to the edge and saw people waving and shouting. He barked at them. Following the edge, he saw more pups playing and bounced on his paws, yipping at them. He wanted to play with them, too.

"We can play with them later, Barney," Master said.

Barney whined and pawed at the invisible wall. Master rubbed his head. "Later." Master grabbed a ball, and Barney tensed, ready to run after it, but Master threw it away. Barney barked, rearing up at the wall, wanting the ball. "It's okay, Barney. There's more." Master threw a few more balls away, and Barney barked each time, racing along the wall to try to get to them. "Fetch, Barney!" Master called, throwing a ball towards Barney this time. Barney jumped for it, missed and raced after it, scrambling to change direction when the ball bounced off something and rolled away again. Several pups joined in the chase, and they ended in a puppy pile, panting. Barney crawled over to Master and lay on his side, legs stretched out as he rested. Master patted his side, stroking him, and Barney closed his eyes, enjoying the feel of it.

A horn blew, making Barney jump, but Master calmed him. "It's nearly the end, Barney," Master whispered. "Sit." Barney whined but pushed himself to sit beside his master. "Good boy." He held a straw to Barney's mouth. "Time to come back." Barney whined. "I know. We can play again later." Master stroked his face. "Come back to me."

Barney finished his drink and leaned his head against his master's chest. Master massaged his head, his neck and his back, and slowly Barney receded and Liam took over. Liam snuggled his head into Troy's neck.

"Are you with me?" Troy asked.

"Mmhmm," Liam answered.

Troy chuckled. "Thirsty?"

"No, I'm good."

A horn sounded three times, and the crowd went wild. The lorry juddered as it stopped.

"Time to get off," Troy said, and Liam couldn't help where his mind went. "Not like that," Troy scolded. "That comes later."

"Definitely." He pulled at his mask, and Troy brushed aside his fingers as he removed it for him. The same with his gloves.

"Do you want to join the parade now?"

Liam lifted his head. "I'd love to walk with everyone, yes."

The second part of this particular parade was a walk, following the same route the floats had taken, but with anyone and everyone who wanted to take part. The crowds could join in, merging with the performers from the initial parade, with lots of music, singing and dancing along the way.

"Let's get ready then. Is Val joining us?"

Liam nodded. "We'll meet him at Book Drunk and then go from there."

"Sounds good. That is, if I'm invited, too?"

Liam smiled up at him. "Of course you are." He leaned in, covering Troy's mouth with his own, ignoring everything around them.

Troy cupped Liam's cheek, holding him close as they explored each other's mouths until they were interrupted.

"Sorry, guys, but we need you to disembark," Lucy said with a chuckle. "Time waits for no one, I'm afraid."

Troy smiled against Liam's lips and pulled back. "That's probably not a bad thing in this situation, Lucy. Thanks." He stood and pulled Liam up, holding him until Liam's legs were strong enough to keep him upright alone.

They climbed down the steps to the ground, and the crowd cheered. Troy's hand found his, and Liam waved at the masses before running a hand through his sweat-dampened hair. They aimed back to their meeting spot.

"How was it?" he asked Troy.

"It was good. I was a little self-conscious in the beginning, but once you started playing, and I had to keep an eye on you, I kind of forgot they were there. Apart from the odd time when they shouted or screamed loud enough to garner my attention." Troy chuckled. "I was worried you were going to jump over the wall when I started throwing those balls into the crowd."

Liam tilted his head, trying to recall how he felt when he was Barney at that point, and nodded. "I wanted those balls and was annoyed I couldn't get them."

"I noticed." Troy pulled him closer, letting go of his hand but sliding his arm around Liam's waist. "Did you enjoy yourself?"

Liam nodded. "Very much." He opened his mouth and then snapped it shut again, fearing to say his thoughts out loud.

"Tell me," Troy murmured.

Liam inhaled. They had discussed so many things, yet nothing at all, but he wanted to take the chance, which surprised him. "It was so much better because it was you as my handler." He waved his hand. "I mean, I trusted you without question. I knew I could let myself completely go because you'd be there to catch me." He chuckled. "Unless I fell off the lorry, then we might have a problem."

Troy pulled him to a stop, and people swarmed around them, continuing their journey. He stared at Liam for a long moment. Long enough that Liam nearly spoke, but then Troy floored him. "I'm falling for you, Liam. I think I have been for months. Every time I saw you at The Den, I fell a little more, and then when I got to know you, when we were practising and when we socialised, I realised just how much I liked you as a person as well as a pup." He sighed. "I've been burnt before. It's why I would've never taken the first step to talk to you. If you hadn't spoken to me in the car park that night, I don't know where we would be. I'd probably still be a total creeper, staring at you every night." He smiled, and Liam's stomach fluttered.

If Liam had to admit it, he could say a similar thing. He'd noticed Troy weeks ago, but he might not have approached him had he not seen him in the car park. Maybe he knew then that Troy would be the one to break through his self-imposed barrier.

"I don't mind you being a creeper, but...yes, I know how you feel. I've travelled for miles to find what I thought I needed, to end up back at home and in the arms of someone I never expected to meet." He swallowed and scratched his head. "I'm..." He chuckled and shook his head. "I'm falling for you, too."

The smile that stretched across Troy's face was so bright, it made the sun look like a dim second-place competitor. Troy caught Liam's nape and dragged him closer, kissing him as if he needed everything Liam could give him.

And maybe he did.

Because it felt the same for Liam.

Twelve

Troy

As Troy's lips touched Liam's, it felt like he was home. That he had found the thing—the person he was supposed to be with and received a similar reaction from them was mind-blowing. He never believed he'd have it because his family... No, he wouldn't think about them. Not now. Today was for celebrating who they were and everything that related to Pride and the LGBTQ+ community. He was no longer hiding who he was. He couldn't if he wanted to be true to himself.

When he pulled back, Liam's eyes were glassy and dilated, and they could do nothing about it. "Later," Troy promised with a final peck on his lips.

They reached Book Drunk a few minutes later, and Val was already bouncing on his toes from what Troy could see.

"You were amazing!" Val said, grabbing Liam for a hug. "So darn cute."

Liam raised his eyebrows. "I'm not cute." But Troy watched his eyes light up at the words.

"You so are," Troy said, kissing his cheek.

Liam's cheeks flushed, and he changed the subject. "Are you ready?"

Val nodded and grabbed some things from behind him. "I've brought flags, tattoo transfers and scarves. Take whatever you want." He shoved some things into Troy's hands. Not willing to be a party pooper, he draped a rainbow scarf around his neck and took a flag.

"Will you put some tattoos on my face?" he asked Liam.

Liam grinned. "Sure."

Troy held still as Liam chose and attached some colourful tattoos to his cheeks. He even stuck one on his forehead, and Troy wondered what he looked like. When Liam finished, Troy turned to the window of Book Drunk and checked his reflection. He had one heart on each cheek and "Love" on his forehead.

"Thank you."

Val took Liam's face into his hands and applied some tattoos for him, far more than what Liam had done with Troy. He looked like he'd put his face in a melted bag of Skittles, as did Val. Troy was glad Liam had gone easy on him, even though Liam looked even cuter with it on.

"Come on! Let's go! It's starting!" Val pushed through the crowd to the barrier and squeezed through as the parade started. Liam and Troy followed him with a laugh and joined the masses as they began the walk through Windsor to celebrate—and defend—their lives.

Various genres of music, a variety of ethnicities and a huge difference of religions, kinks and ages all added to the diversity of the parade, and Troy had never felt more in tune with who he was and where he belonged than he had at that moment. Yes, the community had trials to get through. Yes, they had to face discrimination every day. Yes, they had to decide whether to fight another day or stand up for what they believed in sometimes. But every single person in that parade was someone or had someone who was part of their community. And they were all in that together.

Troy's eyes stung, but he kept the smile on his face, waving his flag above his head and joining in with the singing when he knew the words. There were musicians and drag acts and acrobats and many different walks of life. And as the crowds headed back to Windsor Castle, it amazed him to see rainbow flags of all kinds hanging from the windows of the vast castle. Never, in all his years, had he believed the royals would not only acknowledge the LGBTQ+ members within its family but accept and rejoice with them. But times were changing.

"Are you okay?" Liam asked as the parade ended with another toot of the ear-splitting horn.

Troy nodded. "Perfect," he said. And if his voice cracked, he ignored it. It had been an overwhelming experience to be part of something so monumental.

"Shall we go for something to drink?" Val said, breaking the staring match between Troy and Liam.

Troy raised his eyebrows at Liam. Personally, he didn't want to go anywhere but to bed with Liam, but Val was visiting from Edinburgh, and it wasn't nice to drop him when he'd travelled so far to see his best friend.

Liam licked his lips, broke their gaze and turned to Val. "Can you keep yourself out of trouble for a couple of hours, and we'll meet you for an early dinner?"

Val opened his mouth and then shook his head instead, rolling his eyes. "Sure. Adam wanted me to call him, so I can do that. I'm assuming I'll have the house to myself?" He winked, and Troy cleared his throat, his cheeks heating.

"You will." Liam pulled Val into a hug, whispered something Troy couldn't hear, then grabbed Troy's hand and dragged him away from his best friend.

Troy waved over his shoulder and fell into step beside Liam. "Where are we going?"

"Your house."

That kept him quiet. He knew exactly what Liam needed, and he would be happy to provide it. The journey took them about forty-five minutes on foot because they couldn't get their cars anywhere near the centre of Windsor when such an event was taking place. It was a similar experience whenever the royals had something going on.

Troy unlocked the door and held it open for Liam to enter. Liam kicked off his shoes and waited, tension visible in the way he held himself. Troy took over, allowing Liam to relax into what he knew was coming. Eventually.

"Upstairs. Strip. Kneel by the bed."

Liam's arms pumped as his feet took the steps two at a time, and when he disappeared around the corner, Troy headed for the kitchen. He grabbed two bottles of water and a small carton of apple juice from the fridge. He pulled the punnet of grapes from the basket and put some into a bowl. Resting his hands on the counter, he lowered his head. The day had been wonderful, beyond his imagination, even though he'd seen them on the TV before. Being able to spend it with Liam had made it a hundred times better for him. They'd both announced they were feeling more for each other, and it was a tremendous weight lifted from his shoulders to realise Liam felt the same.

Now, he wanted to show Liam exactly what he meant to Troy.

Tucking the bottles into the crook of his arm, he picked up the juice and the bowl and aimed for the stairs, pausing when he heard the beep of his voicemail. It would be his family. They were the only ones who rang his house phone, and he didn't want to deal with them now. Not when he was on a high note.

Ignoring the sound, he climbed the stairs, making his footfalls heavier to advertise he was on his way. Anticipation curled in his stomach, and his mouth curled as he thought of what he would do to Liam. He couldn't wait to see what noises he could br021ng from him.

Entering his bedroom, he found Liam exactly where he'd asked him to be, and with his head lowered, his hands resting on his thighs, his chest heaving. He wasn't the only one anticipating what they would do.

Troy put everything on the table, except for one bottle of water. He uncapped it and offered it to Liam. "Drink." Liam drank.

"Thank you, Sir."

Troy capped the drink and put it on the table, stepping in front of Liam, hands held loosely at his sides. "I want you to undress me, but...with your eyes closed." Liam's chest hitched.

"Yes, Sir."

Liam closed his eyes and reached his hands forward, sliding his hands up Troy's thighs when he figured out where he was. Having Liam's hands fumbling over him as he tried to unfasten his leather trousers was highly intoxicating, and Troy's cock hardened beneath the zip. A crease formed between Liam's eyebrows while he worked, even as his dick begged for attention, standing upright from between his legs. When Liam got his trousers undone, Troy knelt in front of him, telling him to do his harness. That would take even longer to figure out because, unless Liam had been studying the harness before now, he wouldn't be familiar with how it might come off. But the anticipation would drive them both to the edge of their need.

Liam's fingers trailed along the straps, passing over buckles and catches, both real and fake, and he worked hard to figure it out. Once he knew how, it would be easy. There were two buckles straining across his chest that unfastened, and the rest of the harness slid from his shoulders. When Liam's fingers fiddled with them, fumbling with the fastenings, he made fast progress when he realised they were what he needed.

Blood heated throughout Troy's body, pooling in all the important areas while Liam pushed the harness from his shoulders. It fell to the floor with a soft thud.

"Well done. Shirt."

Liam unfastened the buttons with ease, sending it on the same journey as the harness but with barely a whisper of sound. Troy stood again, his cock straining against the partially open trousers.

"Trousers off."

Liam found the opening he had made earlier, followed around the waistband to where it rested against his back and pushed it over his ass. Leather was never the easiest to remove, especially if there was nothing between the leather and the skin, which, in Troy's case, was true. He'd wanted to feel the leather against him, to give himself something to focus on should the crowds be overwhelming. Now, though, Liam fought with the warm, sweaty material, peeling it from Troy's body. The cool air brushing across the exposed skin was tantalising in itself, but Liam's hands all over him were even more so.

As his cock escaped from the material, Troy hissed, and Liam paused for a second, resuming when Troy didn't stop him. Troy stepped free of the fabric when Liam reached his feet and nudged everything out of the way.

"Eyes stay closed, hands stay on your thighs. Lick." He held his cock at Liam's mouth, and his lover didn't waver in his orders. Liam's mouth opened, and his tongue reached forward, sliding across the head of Troy's shaft. Troy bit his lip, already on the edge from the drawn-out disrobing. "Suck the head."

Liam fitted his mouth around the head, closing his lips just beneath the hood, and used his tongue on both his slit and his frenulum, the nerve endings firing like fireworks up and down Troy's spine. He clenched his hands, needing more but not wanting to rush what they were doing. He let Liam do his thing for a few minutes and then thrust a little deeper into Liam's mouth. He withdrew and paused before repeating the action. Every time he withdrew, Liam increased the suction, his tongue flicking over those nerves. Troy kept at it for as long as he could, but eventually, his restraint snapped, and he pulled himself free.

Troy was grateful he'd chosen the bed he had; it was lower to the ground than more common beds, yet not quite on the floor. "Turn around and place your chest on the bed, keeping your knees on the floor."

Liam scrambled to do as he'd asked, his cock bobbing with his movement, and Troy's mouth watered, wanting it in his mouth. But he would have to wait. As Liam positioned himself, forming a right angle to the ground, Troy ran a hand over his spine and down to his ass, squeezing each cheek.

"Beautiful," he said as pulled the globes apart to see the prize within. Liam's pucker was already pulsing, showing its need to be filled. Troy pushed his cock against the pucker, enticing him with what was to come, but not penetrating yet, even though Liam pushed back with a moan, his hands clenching the covers.

Troy teased them both for several long minutes, running his hands across Liam's skin as his shaft slid between his cheeks, seeking entry. Then he pulled back and stepped away. He collected the lube and a condom from the drawer, then Liam's pup mask from where his clothes lay. He'd love nothing more for Liam to feel free enough to let go and put the mask on if he wished, but he knew it was too much too soon for him. Instead, he placed it in front of his face, close enough for him to scent and see if he opened his eyes, but not touching him in any way.

Stepping back between Liam's legs, he squeezed his ass again, receiving another groan from Liam. "That's it. Let me hear it all." He slicked his fingers and massaged at Liam's pucker before sinking it deep into him. Or rather, allowing Liam's ass to suck it deep. Preparing someone had never been so erotic before, and Troy licked his lips as his shaft pulsed in need. By the time he had three fingers spearing Liam open, Troy's cock leaked as much as a dog's mouth drooled in the summer.

He rolled on a condom and slicked it, pressing it to Liam's entrance. "Are you ready?"

"Yes, Sir," Liam gasped.

"Good." He didn't wait. He couldn't. Slow and steady, he penetrated Liam's ass, sliding deep into his channel until his balls touched Liam's ass. "Fuck," he breathed, bracing his hands on the bed beside Liam's chest.

He lowered his mouth to Liam's shoulder, nipping at the sweat-slicked skin and licking the droplets away. He withdrew a tiny amount, sliding in again and continued this small torture for several minutes, garnering several moans and curses from Liam.

"Please…"

Finally, a response that wasn't withheld. Because now Troy could ask Liam what he wanted. He lowered himself to cover Liam, just as he had done the previous time they'd been together. He rested his hands over Liam's clenched ones and whispered, "Open your eyes."

Liam's eyelids fluttered open, as if the pleasure was already too much for him to witness. He knew the moment Liam saw the mask because his entire body clenched, eliciting a groan from Troy as his ass tightened around his cock. He soothed him by thrusting gently, knowing his cock would be rubbing against the cover beneath him. Liam's eyes were fixed on the mask, but he frowned as if unsure.

"Remember what I said. What happens here is between us, and you only do what feels right to you. If you don't want this, that's fine. But if you do, that's fine, too."

He withdrew in a long slide this time, almost leaving him completely, and then slid back in, undoubtedly rubbing every nerve ending present in his channel. He kept it a slow glide, and when he heard the whine, he almost stopped in surprise, hardly daring to believe Liam was trusting him. He stayed deep inside Liam, pressing kisses to his back and neck, nipping the skin with his teeth, and Liam yipped in response, pushing back.

Troy chuckled. "Impatient." He let go of Liam's hands and braced himself again, then increased his speed and his strength as he slammed inside. The slap of skin-on-skin was music to his ears, and he knew it wouldn't take long for him to come, but he wanted Liam to be free from his concerns. "That's it. Give it to me. I want it all."

Liam whined and writhed and yipped and pushed back against him, seeking his orgasm. Troy loved every move he made, letting him set the pace for now. He couldn't reach beneath him to stroke him off, but he didn't think he needed to if Liam's increasing whines were anything to go by.

But Troy didn't want this to end in the same position it had last time. He wanted them face to face. He pulled free with a growl from Liam, and Troy grinned. Grabbing Liam by the hips, he said, "Get up and on the bed on your back."

Liam did, his body shaking with his need, and when he lay down, his cock was purple and straining. Troy knew how it felt. Immediately, he hooked Liam's legs over his arms and bent him in half, his cock finding the hole he needed to bring them to their completion. He lowered his head as he sank inside, tasting Liam's lips and tongue, wanting everything of him inside Troy, too. The idea of Liam's dick inside him was more arousing than it had been before, and he started at a frenetic pace, taking them higher and higher. Liam's eyes darkened, the pupils blowing as wide as his mouth when his cock pulsed his release onto his stomach and chest. How Troy had kept himself from coming before then, he didn't know, but with Liam over the edge, Troy picked up his pace and, a few thrusts later, followed him.

He buried his face in Liam's neck, letting his breathing come back to normal. He didn't want to move, but he needed to remove the condom. Although when he made a move, Liam slipped his arms around his back and held him tightly, not letting him leave. Troy settled back against him for a moment until Liam's chest hitched. Was he crying?

Thirteen

LIAM

Liam couldn't stop the tears from streaming from his eyes into his hair, but it wasn't because he was sad. If anything, he felt free. Freer than he had ever felt, and it had everything to do with Troy allowing him to be whoever he needed to be.

He didn't want to be a pup when he was having sex, but he wanted to be free to make the pup noises. When he had done it with past partners, they'd freaked out, thinking he was into animals, which couldn't be farther from the truth. He needed just to be able to let his body decide how he reacted without having someone tell him he was wrong or a freak or anything else along those lines. He couldn't help how his body reacted, and Troy had accepted him as he was, without reservations.

Troy lifted his head. "Are you okay?" His cock slipped free. "Hold that thought. Let me deal with this for a second."

He rolled free, removing the condom and throwing it into the bin Liam knew was beside the bed. Then he came back and positioned himself as he had been, wrapping Liam in his arms. "Now. What's wrong?"

Liam stroked a finger over Troy's cheek, trying to figure out how to say what he wanted to say. In the end, he repeated his thoughts.

Troy smiled. "I'm glad I can give you that. I never, ever believed it had anything to do with the animal aspect. I'm not into animals, either, but I love that you can be free. Barney is as much a part of you as the rest of you. It makes sense to have him need to be vocal when something is happening. Be it sex, a shouting match or any event that heightens your emotions. It's not wrong."

"Thank you," Liam said, his voice feeling like it was working through sandpaper. He closed his eyes.

"We can stay here for as long as you want to, but you might want to message Val and let him know we'll be late," Troy murmured after a few minutes.

Liam inhaled, held it and released it, and with it released months or years of pent-up tension. It wouldn't stop his insecurities from rising on occasion, but it would help that day, at the very least. He could spend the evening with his friend and Troy and enjoy the festivities, which were due to go on late into the night.

"Can I shower before we go?" he asked.

"Of course. Would you like some help washing your back?" Troy winked.

Liam laughed. "I doubt that will be any quicker, but sure."

It wasn't quicker, and in the end, Val cursed them for being nearly an hour late. "It's a good job I could talk to Adam while I waited."

"How is he doing?" Liam asked after ordering them a round of drinks at the bar they had chosen. The same bar he and Val had attended the previous night for the drag show. That evening's entertainment was a local band, which was made up of gay, lesbian and transsexual members. And afterwards, if they lasted that long, there was a karaoke session. He'd love to see how Troy was at singing.

"He's fine. It was a shame he had to work, but he said he'll take a holiday next time and come with me. Or maybe you can come up to Edinburgh instead?" Val said hopefully.

Liam chuckled. "I'm happy to visit. You know I love Edinburgh." He turned to Troy. "Have you ever been?"

Troy nodded. "When I was younger. Family working holiday."

Liam understood the undercurrents of those words, and he squeezed Troy's thigh. "We can make new memories. Val knows all the 'best' places." Liam used air quotes because he was sure Val had no sense of taste. All Liam had to think about was the many times they'd ended up in seedy-looking places to know he'd done no research whatsoever.

Val backhanded his shoulder, and Liam laughed. "I'm not that bad!"

Liam raised his eyebrows. "I'll let Adam answer that question when you next ask him."

Val narrowed his eyes at him and then smirked. "So, Troy. What do you see in this lug?"

Troy's mouth twitched. "I see a well-motivated, highly intelligent businessman with mischievous pup tendencies."

Val snorted into his drink. "He's definitely got you pegged." Val covered his mouth with his hand. "Wrong wording."

Liam cuffed the back of Val's head as he joined in the laughter. "Shut up before you ruin everything."

Luckily for them all, the music started. Liam spent an enjoyable evening with two men who meant a lot to him. The only way it would've been better was if Robert and Henry could've joined them, but there was only so much royals could get away with, after all.

They grabbed a taxi to take them home, but as Val climbed in, Troy pulled Liam around to face him in the open door.

"I'm going to head home. You need to sleep and spend the weekend with Val."

"You can stay with us, too."

Troy shook his head. "No. We've had a lot of emotions and announcements over the last few days, and I want you to relax and talk with Val without watching what you say around me." Troy cupped his face. "I want you. More than anything. But I also want you to be sure. I don't want you to rush into anything."

Liam rested his forehead against Troy's and closed his eyes. "Okay. Can I call you tomorrow, though?"

"I'd be sad if you didn't." Troy kissed him, chaste and soft. "I want you to get some rest."

"Yes, Sir," Liam whispered.

Troy pulled back, stroking a finger over his cheek. "Sleep well."

Liam smiled, but he wanted to pull Troy into the car with him. That in itself told him Troy was right. They needed to take a breather and make sure their hormones or whatever weren't making the wrong decisions for them.

"Can we make plans for this week?"

Troy chuckled. "When you call tomorrow, we'll arrange something." He leaned down and said goodbye to Val and stepped back from the car. "Have a good evening."

Liam climbed in and shut the door, watching as Troy disappeared.

"You've got it bad," Val teased.

"Maybe," he replied distractedly.

Did Troy regret what they'd said to each other? Is that why he didn't want to stay with him? Liam shook his head internally. No, Troy wasn't like that. He wasn't like all the others. Troy wanted him to be himself. To be true to how he felt inside. To let both sides of his life work in tandem with each other. He wouldn't make Liam believe all that if he hadn't a vested interest in something more with him. That was Liam's insecurities talking.

Val nudged him, and Liam realised they were home. "Sorry."

"No problem. Let's grab a drink."

Even though it was Liam's apartment, Val led the way, settling Liam on the sofa with a glass of water and snuggling up beside him.

"Talk."

As Liam had done many years before, he let everything out. All the little voices, what Troy had said to him about being himself, the issues he was having with believing it whenever Troy wasn't there. He talked for over an hour, and Val let him, only asking questions when he needed confirmation. When he finally finished, his throat was hoarse despite the numerous drinks he'd finished.

"You're in love."

The plain statement reached where nothing else could've, but Liam shook his head. "No, I can't be."

Val smirked. "Yes, you can. I can see it when you're with him. You look at him with stars in your eyes. You move closer as if you can't bear to be too far away from him. The whole time we've been here, you must've checked your phone twenty times. If that's not a sign of being in love, then I'm not in love with Adam."

"Yes, you are! Don't say that!"

Val placed a hand on Liam's arm. "I *am* in love with him, and that's why I know. You are exactly how I was when I met him."

Liam stared at the coffee table. Was he? Could it really be as easy as that? As easy as allowing himself to love? Surely there were avalanches to avoid, shark-infested waters to swim and rickety bridges over an infinite drop to cross before settling into love?

When he thought about not seeing Troy again, a weight pressed on his chest. Troy made everything brighter, brought everything into focus. Liam could honestly say he appeared to have been living in a slightly blurry world all this time. The only pinprick of focus had been Lora and Val, and then Paul. And Robert and Henry. And now Lula and Troy. His world had slowly expanded without him even realising it.

"I think you're right," Liam murmured.

Val leaned closer, cupping his hand behind his ear. "Sorry? What was that? Can you say that a bit louder for those in the back of the house?"

Liam chuckled and shoved him back. "Nope. That's all you get."

"Shame. I doubt you'll ever say it again." Val stared at him, a small smile playing around his lips. "If it's any consolation, he's as in love with you as you are with him. And love looks good on you both."

Liam closed his eyes and grimaced, knowing he'd never hear the end of it. Instead of arguing with his best friend, he stood. "I'm going to bed."

"Say goodnight to Troy for me."

Liam ducked into the shower for a quick rinse and then settled into bed, bringing up Troy's message thread.

LIAM: *Goodnight, sleep tight, make sure the pups don't bite.*

He waited, and a couple of minutes later, he received a reply.

TROY: *Sleep tight, sleep well, wishing you sweet dreams as well.*
LIAM: *You're supposed to have two different words that rhyme.*
TROY: *Give me a break. That was on the fly.*
LIAM: *I suppose it'll do.*
TROY: *Glad you approve. I'll do better next time.*
LIAM: *Are you in bed?*
TROY: *I am. Are you?*
LIAM: *I am. I'm going to sleep like I told you I would.*
TROY: *Good boy. Call me tomorrow. x*
LIAM: *I will. Goodnight. x*
TROY: *Goodnight, sweetheart. x*

Liam set the phone on the bedside table and plugged it in to charge overnight. Then he settled down, pulling the covers to his waist. It was too warm for anything else, but he enjoyed the comfort of a cover, even in hot weather. He stared at the ceiling for a moment, then closed his eyes, hoping to find the sweet dreams Troy wished upon him.

And he did, but he also woke several times throughout the night, reaching for someone who wasn't there. How long had he slept alone? And how many times had he slept with Troy? The maths didn't add up to why he was needing Troy next to him for him to be able to sleep.

When morning came, he groaned, pulling the pillow back over his head to block out the sun. But after remembering what Troy had said about the sunshine making people feel better if they woke to it shining on them, he removed the pillow but kept his eyes closed while he adjusted to the bright light. After a few moments of blinking to get his eyes to stay open, he checked the clock and groaned a second time. He'd been in bed for around six hours, but asleep for about three. He didn't want to waste a moment, though.

He pushed himself upright and scrubbed at his face, brushing away the sleep. Val was leaving that afternoon, and he wanted to spend the day with him. Troy had been right about telling Liam to stay with Val instead of going with Troy. He always put Liam first.

Val's announcement came back to him, and Liam smiled. He loved Troy. It felt right. Even though he had been pushing for this type of relationship, he hadn't been able to see it when it was right in front of him. He shook his head and chuckled, heading for the bathroom. He had a fun day planned for them, and Val would love it.

Six hours later, after physically dragging Val from bed to start the day at a supposedly ungodly hour, Liam stood on the train station platform, hugging Val within an inch of his life.

"I'll be back before you know it. It only takes around five hours on a train, and we can fly even quicker. We'll arrange to visit each other more often. I'll make sure of it."

Liam could hear the sadness in Val's voice, and he couldn't have him like that for the entire journey. "You'll have to come back. Lula will never forgive you if you don't visit her."

Val pulled back, laughing. "That little beauty already has you all wrapped around her little finger, and I beg anyone to try to change my mind."

"You don't need to. She's done the same for you."

"Hell, yes!"

They laughed. The tannoy announced Val's train was pulling in, and Liam exhaled. He loved having Val with him, but he didn't begrudge his life in Edinburgh with the man he was made for and was made for him. Val headed closer to the edge while Liam stayed where he was.

"Make sure you go straight to Troy after this. You have to tell him you love him," Val shouted across the space, causing more than one person to stare at them.

Liam closed his eyes, shaking his head, but he nodded.

"Promise me!"

Knowing Val wouldn't get on the train until he gave his promise—even though he was tempted to not do it to make him stay—he called out his promise. Val hooted and fist-pumped the air as the door closed, separating them for however many days, weeks or months it would be until they saw each other again.

As Liam wandered back to his car, he considered just turning up on Troy's doorstep. Troy hadn't said he wasn't welcome, but he had said they needed a breather to think everything through. Was fourteen hours enough time? It had to be because Liam needed to see him.

He aimed the car towards Troy's home, and once again, marvelled at the size of it. He could understand why Troy had said he wouldn't have bought it if he'd had the choice because it wasn't Troy at all. He'd done a fantastic job of making the inside reflect more of how Liam saw Troy, but the house itself was too big and too fancy when Troy wasn't like that at all. He needed a smaller place, an understated beauty that could be moulded into what he needed, rather than space for more people than Troy would ever want in the house at the same time.

He parked in the driveway, the crunch of the tyres announcing his presence—well, *a* presence. Troy wouldn't know it was him until he looked out of the window or opened the door.

Whether that was a good thing would be written on Troy's face when he saw him.

Liam rang the doorbell and shoved his hands into his pockets. There was no sign of life. Was he even home? His car was there, but maybe he'd gone for a walk. Then he saw a shadow move behind the glass of the door, and it opened with a flourish. Liam knew immediately that Troy wasn't happy. The shine that beamed from his spirit was dulled, and his expression was tight. What had happened?

"Is everything okay?" Liam asked, but Troy lifted a finger to his mouth, asking for quiet. Liam frowned as Troy glanced to the side and grimaced.

"Yes, Mother." Troy beckoned him in, but Liam wanted to run when he realised Troy was speaking with his mother. He stepped inside, though, staying near the door when Troy headed down the hallway and disappeared. "It wasn't intentional…" his voice trailed off. Troy's head appeared again, and he waved for Liam to join him.

Liam waved his hands to say no or continue or whatever he was trying to get across, but Troy frowned and strode closer.

"Mother, there's someone at the door and they're not leaving. Let me put you on mute while I get rid of them."

That hurt. Liam swallowed and lowered his eyes.

"It'll only be for a few seconds, Mother. You don't really want me shouting in your ear, do you?" Troy nodded and pressed a button in his ear, removing the earpiece and putting it on the table. "That wasn't about you," he whispered before he dragged Liam into his arms and kissed the ever-loving-heck out of him.

Liam lost himself in the feel of Troy—his mouth, his tongue, his hands, his body—and when he came back to himself, he had no idea how long they'd been in the embrace. Troy rested his forehead against Liam's.

"I'm sorry about that. I needed you. And you turned up at the perfect time."

Liam looked into Troy's eyes and saw the truth. He did need him. "Troy…" Was now the right time?

Troy lifted his head and smiled at Liam, encouraging him with his expression. "What?"

Liam inhaled, deciding to take the chance. "I love you."

Fourteen

Troy

Troy stared at Liam, unable to believe what Liam had said. He studied his face, checking he'd heard what he thought he had. "Say it again," he whispered.

Liam licked his lips, scratched his head, and then refocused on Troy. "I love you, Troy. I have plenty more words I could say, but that's it in its final form. I love you."

Troy slammed his mouth on Liam's, catching his gasp of surprise, and held his head as he plundered his mouth. When he pulled back, he breathed hard and met Liam's gaze. "I love you." He shook his head and huffed a laugh. "You cannot understand how perfect timing you have." He stepped back and threaded their fingers together. "I have to finish this phone call with my mother, and it's not pleasant. Will you stay?"

"If you want me to, of course."

Troy picked up his phone and instead of slipping the earpiece back into his ear, he put the call on speakerphone, hearing his mother's side of the phone call, where she cursed him up and down the country for taking so long. Inhaling, he stared into Liam's eyes and pressed the unmute button.

"Sorry, Mother. They didn't want to leave."

"Next time, don't answer the door! I don't have all hours of the day to spend talking to you, you know. We have work to do. Gina has to practise before her show. You're so uncaring sometimes."

"I apologise. It won't happen again." He tugged Liam towards his office, needing the comfort of his aquarium while he finished the call.

"You're right, it won't." She huffed. "Now, as I said, I don't appreciate checking on the home news and finding you in the centre of the...festivities there. I don't see how this can shine a good light on Gina's career."

Troy palmed his forehead, rubbing in gentle circles. "It's not about Gina, Mother. It's about me. I'm part of that community. I want to be part of it."

"But how does that help Gina?"

Knowing his mother wouldn't budge on it unless it was something that could help his sister, he mouthed an apology to Liam and said, "She will be able to reach more people if she shows she's inclusive of all communities. If you focus only on some, you won't reach everyone. Having a gay brother is a way to reach the LGBTQ+ community, especially here at home."

"Hmm." She was silent for a moment. "Well, I don't like you doing it without our consent. Next time, ask first."

He wasn't agreeing to that. "I hope everything is going well there."

"Gina is hitting her performance targets and practising regularly. She has dinner with some important people here in two weeks, so we're extending our stay to accommodate it."

"Of course."

"Make sure you stay out of trouble, Troy. Gina doesn't need the bad publicity."

His mother didn't say goodbye, she just ended the call, and Troy threw it on the table and sagged back, closing his eyes. "Sorry about that."

"Is she always like that?"

Troy snorted and glanced at Liam. "That was her on a good day. Gina performed well last night, so she was in a good mood."

Liam's eyebrows rose, and he jerked back as if someone had hit him. "Good mood? Seriously?"

Troy nodded and sighed. "I told you I'm the black sheep of the family. I stay out of the spotlight as much as possible. Being in the festival wasn't my brightest idea, though I did think I would be able to get away with it as they're in Australia. I never thought she'd check the news in Windsor to keep track of things."

"Or keep track of you."

Troy conceded that with a tilt of his head. "So... You love me?"

Liam chuckled, covering his mouth with his hand. Then he bit his lip and stared at Troy. "I do. Val made me realise it last night and made me promise to tell you straight away."

"You should've waited until he left. I don't want you missing your time with him."

Liam grinned. "Like we did yesterday?" He chuckled when Troy closed his eyes, reminded of taking Liam away from his best friend for a couple of hours. "It's fine. I took him to the train before I came here. I probably should've done some big announcement for you to show you how much I love you, even after such a short amount of time, but I drove straight here."

Troy sat upright, lifting his knee to the sofa so he could see Liam better. "You are a marvel, Liam Sawyer, and you don't even know it." Troy smiled, their pronouncements making his decision easier. "There's someone I want you to meet."

"As long as it's not a secret boyfriend or, potentially, your mother, I'm happy to meet anyone you want to introduce me to."

Troy chuckled. "You have a while before you have to meet my parents." He stood, pulling Liam up. "I'll drive."

"Are you not going to tell me who I'm meeting?" Liam asked as he clicked his seatbelt closed.

"No. I want to see your reaction when we get there."

Liam frowned. "I don't know if I like the idea of that."

Troy laughed. "I promise it's nothing that will cause you bodily harm. Unless you hurt me, then all bets are off."

Liam snorted. "I'll be on my best behaviour then."

"Yes, keep Barney on a short leash." Troy shook his head. "I'm only messing with you. You behave however you want to behave."

As they drove through Windsor, Liam commented on the different houses he had done landscaping jobs for, and it occurred to Troy that Liam knew quite a few people through his business, but not many he would call friends. Would their world open up more now they were together, officially? He'd have to wait and see.

"I did a job around here not long ago," Liam said. "A lovely pond that needed some tender loving care. The elderly lady was lovely. She'd not long lost her husband and wanted something made in his memory."

Troy's breath hitched. No way. It couldn't be. "That sounds wonderful."

"It looks great, even if I say so myself. Surprisingly, she didn't seem lonely." Liam tilted his head as he stared out of the windscreen. "I would've thought she would be having lost her husband."

"Did she have other family?" Troy was fishing, but he only had to wait a few more moments to see if his hunch was correct.

"She mentioned that she didn't see her family very often, although had a grandson who visited plenty."

Troy shook his head. Un-fucking-believable. He pulled up at the house, and Liam smiled, then frowned and glanced at Troy.

"How did you know which house it was?"

Troy's mouth twitched. "I'd like you to meet my grandmother."

Liam's eyes widened, his gaze darting over the house and back to Troy again. "Mrs Corrigan is your grandmother? You're her grandson?"

"That's usually how it works."

"Why didn't you tell me?"

Troy put his hands up. "I didn't know you were the one who'd done it. It was only when you mentioned what you'd done for her and her situation that I realised we had a link."

"Holy crap! I've already met your family!"

Troy laughed and climbed out of the car. Liam followed, and they wandered up the pathway to the door. Troy put the key in the door and unlocked it, having insisted his grandmother locked the door, even when she was in the house.

"Nan, it's me!"

"Troy, dear! I wondered when I'd get to see you next."

Troy's grandmother, Mrs Eugenie Corrigan, came into the hallway with a shuffle. She was getting on in years now, but she was as fit as the next person, though she hid it well. The grief she undoubtedly felt at the loss of Troy's grandfather was never visible on her face, except when she spoke of him, which they did regularly.

"Liam! How lovely to see you again!" She glanced between them. "Well, when Troy said he was interested in someone called Liam, I hadn't believed it possible he meant the one I had considered setting him up with."

Troy laughed, holding his stomach. "Really, Nan?"

Eugenie nodded her head. "He's perfect for you, Troy. It was only because he said he'd been hurt that I didn't push." She smiled at Liam and held out her arms. "Come here, Liam. Let me welcome you to the family the right way."

Liam glanced at Troy, who nodded, then walked into his grandmother's arms. Eugenie whispered something to him, and Liam nodded when he pulled back. She patted his cheek, then winked at Troy.

"Are you a dog lover, Liam?"

"Yes, Mrs Corrigan. Why do you ask?"

"If that quote didn't talk about dogs, then I would be truly confused." She gestured to his T-shirt, which said, "*You threw it. You go fetch it.*"

"It's definitely about dogs," Troy said. "He has probably hundreds of them."

"Come on. We're wasting drinking time," Eugenie said.

Liam raised his eyebrows as she disappeared as quickly as she'd appeared. "Drinking time?" he whispered.

Troy snorted. "Tea. She means tea."

Liam blew out a breath and laughed. "I can't believe it."

"I know. What're the chances?" He stared at Liam. "I don't think we ever had the option to say no to this, did we?" When Liam frowned, he added, "Fate seems to have been throwing us together, no matter what."

"And I couldn't be happier about it," Liam said, threading their fingers together.

"Boys! Come on!" Eugenie called.

· · · · ● · ● · · ·

After spending a couple of hours with his grandmother, they headed back to Troy's house, and Troy led Liam straight up to his bedroom, undressing them both as they went. Instead of shoving Liam onto the bed and mounting him with the need bubbling inside him, Troy lay on his back and beckoned Liam to straddle him.

"I want you to ride me."

He'd dreamt of that a few nights ago and hadn't been able to get the images out of his head. He wanted to see Liam undulating on top of him as he reached for his climax.

He grabbed the lube and a condom from the drawer, placing them within reach. Liam climbed over him, their cocks nudging against each other as he leaned down for a kiss Troy would never deny him. They were both already hard and leaking. Just the anticipation of what was to come had Troy's body readying for Liam.

Their lips sipped and nipped until Liam pulled away, gasping and grinding his lower body over Troy's groin.

"Let me prep you."

"Quickly! Please!" Liam whined, and Troy loved that he was more comfortable with his pup noises now.

Troy grabbed the lube and slicked his fingers, sliding them behind Liam to get him ready. He worked as quickly as he could without skimping on the stretching. He refused to hurt him if it could be prevented.

"Please," Liam growled.

Troy tore at the condom wrapper with his teeth and rolled it on blindly, slicking it with the leftover lube on his hands. He gripped Liam's ass cheek with one hand

and held his cock to Liam's pucker with the other. The slightest pressure had Liam groaning and pushing down on him. Liam worked his ass up and down a few times before Troy slid in fully with a moan. His hands left his cock and squeezed Liam's cheeks while Liam rolled his hips as he adjusted.

Troy lifted his head to catch Liam's lips with his teeth, dragging his head down for a kiss. When Liam rolled his hips again, their mouths gaped, and they just breathed into each other. Liam braced himself on his palm and reached for his shaft, wrapping his hand around it and stroking the straining length. Troy clenched Liam's ass and rocked his own hips upwards, sliding deeper inside Liam's channel.

He closed his eyes and dropped his head back, despite wanting to see everything. Liam dropped down as Troy pushed up, slowly and gently, not wanting to rush. The sweat had already started beading on both their skins, their bodies sliding easier against each other.

Troy transferred his hands to Liam's waist, picking up the pace a little, and Liam's stroking hand increased, too.

"Ah, fuck," Liam breathed with each thrust.

Troy held him still for a moment and quickened his own hips, teasing them as much as he could manage without going over the edge. He wanted this to last.

Liam dropped his forehead to Troy's. "Ohhh." He panted. "Fuck."

Then Troy slowed down again and let Liam sit upright, which pushed Troy even deeper. Liam's head dropped back, the long line of his throat visible and sexy as hell. Troy made a note to explore that area later. His gaze continued down his sweat-slicked body to his cock, the head poking through Liam's fist as he stroked. Troy wanted that. He pushed Liam's hand aside and replaced it with his own, even as he wished he could reach it with his mouth.

Liam leant back, putting his hands on the bed between Troy's legs, stretching his body taut. "Oh, fuck!" he said as he worked his hips backwards onto Troy's cock and forwards into Troy's fist. "Fuck. Oh!"

The noises he made were incredible, and Troy slid his free hand up Liam's stomach and chest, flicking his nipple while he thrust and stroked. As Liam got louder and louder, Troy's body heated further. Liam pushed upright again and rolled forward to kiss Troy, even as their hips worked towards their ultimate goal. Troy gripped Liam's hips and thrust hard, pulling Liam down as he did, over and over again.

"Fucking hell, Liam." Troy groaned into his neck, wrapping his arms around Liam's waist and holding him tight against him while his hips pistoned. He could feel Liam's cock rubbing between them, and Troy thrust as hard and as fast as he could. The slap of their skin joined with the melody of Liam's cries, and despite his limbs burning with the need to stop, he continued until Liam tensed and shouted his release.

Troy fell over barely a second later, and he kept up the thrusting, though slowed it down some, bringing them down gently.

Liam collapsed against his chest, and Troy slid his cock free, dealing with the condom blindly so he didn't have to move the man. Although, they would have to move sooner rather than later; otherwise, they'd be stuck to each other. Instead, he slid his arms around Liam, holding him, breathing in his scent and feeling Liam's breath on his chest. He would not change locations for all the money in the world.

"Troy?"

"Hmm?"

"I love you."

Troy smiled and kissed Liam's head. "I love you."

He let Liam rest for a few moments before he manoeuvred him to the side so Troy could get a cloth. As it was, he had to wash his stomach as Liam's release had dried. He wet a cloth with warm water, hoping it was easier to remove from Liam, and nudged the man over onto his back.

"I'm just washing you," he said with a smile when Liam batted at his hand. "You can't sleep for too long, anyway. You need food." As if on cue, Liam's stomach growled. "Told you."

"Sleepy," Liam said, opening one eye. "Someone kept me awake last night." Troy frowned at him, and Liam chuckled. "You," he said. "You were in my dreams, and every time I woke up, you weren't beside me."

Troy's heart skipped a beat, and his stomach swooped as he finally understood how far he had fallen for this amazing man. He threw the cloth into the washing basket and tugged the covers from beneath Liam, dragging them over him once he had them clear. Then he climbed in beside him and pulled him into his arms.

"Then sleep. I'll wake you in a little while."

Liam snuggled into him, and Troy kissed his temple. He rested his cheek against Liam's head and closed his eyes. He wouldn't sleep himself; he'd watch over him and make sure he fed him soon. If he slept now, they'd probably be asleep for hours, and it was Troy's job to take care of Liam.

With everything that had happened that weekend, Troy would've thought he would be exhausted, but he wasn't. He had energy to burn, and he couldn't wait to spend more time with Liam, either man and man or handler and pup. Their lives seem to be able to slot into each other's without problems, and if that didn't show how well they went together, nothing would.

And as for Liam being the landscaper to do his grandmother's garden, that was mind-blowing. Troy had never thought to ask about who had done it, and he'd never volunteered what Liam did as a career to his grandmother before. Such small bites of information that could've changed the way everything worked out.

But at that moment, he was content to hold Liam in his arms and cross any and all bridges later. If Elton hadn't paired them together for the event, would they have reached the place they were in? He had to hope they would have. It might just have taken them longer to get there.

Fate takes no prisoners, it seemed.

Liam's stomach growled, and Troy laughed.

"I'm hungry," Liam murmured.

"Then let's get you fed," Troy said.

"I'm too comfortable."

Troy squeezed him tighter. "I'll treat you to dinner in bed. Just this once, though."

"You're the best," Liam mumbled, snuggling into the pillow Troy had left.

Troy shook his head and stared at him, never wanting the man to leave. He leaned down and whispered, "I love you," and then pulled on some boxers so he didn't burn himself while he made dinner.

He could get used to having Liam in his bed every day. And he hoped he would.

Fifteen

LIAM

Three months later

Liam cradled Lulu to his chest as they wandered through the corridors of Windsor Castle. He had been there a couple of times, but this was the first time that his sister, her husband, and little Lulu had been there—not that Lulu would remember it. Patrick had insisted on meeting the newest family member so they could introduce her to Kieren as well. He wasn't sure if there was more to it than that, but he refused to waste an opportunity to see his friends.

Troy walked beside him, a small smile gracing his lips. He found it amusing that Liam wanted to hold Lulu when her mother was right beside them, but Liam found comfort in the tiny, warm body held close to his.

"They're here!" someone shouted from down the corridor, and Liam couldn't withhold his chuckle, interrupting Lulu's nap. She settled back down quickly when he shushed and jiggled her.

Robert led them into a spacious room, where every royal family member appeared to be waiting for them. Liam smiled when Henry waved across at them.

"The little princess is napping," Lora said, "but she needs to wake up; otherwise, I'll have hell later."

A ripple of laughter ran around the room, and Patrick stepped forward. "I'm more than happy to be the mean uncle and wake her." He held out his arms, and Liam didn't hesitate to pass her over. He'd discussed this with Lora and Paul beforehand, and they were more than happy to share the love with the royal family.

As Patrick held Lulu comfortably in his arms, he smiled down at her, and Liam believed his instincts had been correct—Patrick wanted a little one of his own. And by the looks of the other princes, they all had similar feelings. Would there be some little princes or princesses running around the halls of Windsor Castle soon? Liam hoped there would be.

"Kieren, look at her," Patrick said, carefully settling beside his boyfriend on a comfortable-looking sofa. "Isn't she beautiful?"

Liam could see Lora preen beside him, and he chuckled, nudging her. "You make beautiful kids, sis, and you know it."

Lora giggled. "Mixing our genes was a good idea." She thumbed over her shoulder at Paul. "Maybe we can do it again?" She raised her eyebrows in her husband's direction, who immediately grinned. "Give me a few months to recover first," she said.

Troy sat on another sofa, deep in conversation with Robert. They had become firm friends, as had Troy and Patrick, especially with their love for music. Liam's man would start working with Patrick in a couple of weeks, and though Troy's parents disapproved, Troy didn't care. He'd cut as many ties with them as he could, ever since they'd had a blowout argument when they'd returned from Australia. Gina stayed out of it, and she and Troy were getting along, albeit carefully. They'd had a heart to heart and Gina had told them she hadn't wanted to be as big of a star as she was, but she hadn't much of a choice. But she enjoyed it, so she couldn't complain too much. And as much as Troy didn't love the house he was in, he and his parents had agreed for him to keep the house, regardless of their...separation.

It had made things easier on them all because they didn't have to be careful of their words. They could carry on as normal. Well, as normal as things could be for a landscaper and an estate agent when they were part of a famous family as well as friends with the royal family. It had been a shock when reporters had started showing up at random places when they were working or having fun, but they were told they would get used to it.

Liam settled into the seat beside Troy, resting his hand on his thigh, which Troy covered with his own hand while still conversing with Robert. Liam watched Patrick and Kieren as they stared down at Lulu—who was awake and kicking her arms and legs by this point—lost in their own little bubble. He would love to see some little royal family members running around the place, but it wasn't his place to say anything.

"I think you might be right," Troy whispered in his ear.

"About what?"

Troy raised his eyebrows. "You know what."

Liam chuckled. "Maybe. It won't be a quick result, though. Especially with who they are. Who could they trust with something so big?"

"True. It would take time to find someone who would be willing to not sell their story to the highest bidder after they helped."

Liam's heart skipped a beat, and he glanced at his sister, who was deep in conversation with Henry, though kept glancing across the room at her daughter. Being a surrogate was a big thing for anyone, but for the royal family...enormous. Was that something Lora would consider? Was it something she would want to do? He'd have to speak to her about it because it wasn't a decision to take lightly, but he had a feeling she had already thought about it to some degree.

"Where is this beauty I've been told so much about?" a voice said.

Liam glanced over his shoulder to see King Andrew entering with Kean and Kendal, his partners. Andrew—as he'd insisted Liam and Troy call him—strode over to Patrick and leaned down, smiling at Lulu, who immediately reached for him. Andrew chuckled and picked her up, holding her in front of his face so she could grab at him. When she had a good grip on his beard,

Andrew laughed and rested her against his chest, not even trying to get her to let go.

"You truly are a beauty, Miss Lulu." He glanced around and stopped on Lora and Paul. "Thank you for bringing her. It might get some of these lugs to get into the parenting mindset. I officially offer you any of these people, including Freddie and Damon, who aren't here, as babysitters whenever you need them. They'll need the practice."

Gasps, mutters and groans echoed around the room, and Liam snorted. None of them were getting out of it, though Liam bet none of them truly wanted to.

Troy slid his arm around Liam's shoulders, and Liam dropped his head onto Troy's shoulder. Contentment flowed through him, and he couldn't believe where his life had taken him. He would always be sad that his parents had been taken from them so soon, but he would be forever grateful that his life had been pushed onto the path it had. He wouldn't be where he was that day unless everything that happened *had* happened.

Troy pressed his lips to Liam's forehead, and Liam sighed, watching the royal family fawn over Liam's niece. Lulu would never want for anything because she had more uncles than she would ever need, which would, when she was older, ruin her social life. Liam smiled. He wouldn't be the only one looking after her as she grew.

"You okay?" Troy asked.

"Yep. Just imagining what Lulu will think of having I don't know how many uncles when she becomes a teenager."

Troy paused and then snorted. "Oh god. She'll kill us all."

"Probably."

They settled into comfortable conversations, the minutes and hours flying by until it was time for them to head out. Lora and Paul needed to get Lulu home, and Liam and Troy were heading to The Den. They were meeting up with Nomad and Dodo for a playdate—if it could even be called that when they were always there together, anyway.

Andrew came over to them and cleared his throat. "I would like to extend an invitation for you to join Club Royal."

Liam gaped at him. He'd heard rumours, but as no one had mentioned anything about it, he'd assumed it was just that. Rumours. Henry and Robert had never indicated they were part of it, and they'd played at The Den plenty of times, as had George, Timothy and Eddie.

"I... I..." He glanced at Troy, unable to figure out what to say.

Troy's mouth twitched. "I think what he's trying to say is that we'd love to."

Andrew smiled. "Great. There are a few checks to go through before we can officially accept you, but I don't see that being a problem. I'll let Henry get in contact with you to sort out those details, and then we can see what we can do. We'd love to have you."

"You really own Club Royal?" Liam said finally.

"Woohoo! Pay up!" George shouted, holding out his hand.

Patrick, Christian and Kieren slapped something into George's palm with a groan, and Liam raised his eyebrows at Robert. Robert rolled his eyes.

"George said you didn't have a clue they owned Club Royal, but the other three said you would have some idea."

Liam shook his head, still shocked by the announcement. "I honestly thought they were rumours, and that's all."

"That's the idea," Andrew said. "Our NDAs are watertight, and so far, we've had no one who has breached them enough to cause issues. Rumours are okay, but the truth is not."

Liam heard the warning behind the words and nodded. "I'd love to see the place."

Henry bounced up. "You will *love* the pet play area. It will blow your mind."

Liam smiled. "Sounds amazing."

"I'll call you in the week to figure it out, and then we can make a date to go together," Henry said.

They said their goodbyes and headed for the exit with Kieren as a guide while he cradled Lulu in his arms. The man reluctantly gave Lulu back when they reached the doors, and Liam shook hands with him.

"She'll grow up protected," Kieren promised to Lora and Paul. "You won't ever have to worry about that."

"Thank you," Lora said, pulling Kieren in for a hug. "You don't understand how much that means to us."

Kieren swallowed. "Actually, I do."

It was then Liam remembered that Kieren had lost his entire family in a plane crash years earlier, leaving him with no one. He would understand what it was like for them having lost their parents, and Liam wanted to thank him again but didn't want to bring too much attention to it. He'd have to tell Lora about it.

They separated in the driveway, climbing into different cars, and Liam sighed as he settled into the passenger seat.

"Are you sure you're okay?" Troy asked as he manoeuvred through the streets of Windsor towards The Den.

"Yeah." He explained about Kieren. "They always say like attracts like. It must be true for more than relationships. Friends do the same, it seems."

"Everyone comes into your life when they're needed. Sometimes, they stay forever; sometimes, they're a brief whirlwind who leave again."

"You're not leaving," Liam stated.

Troy chuckled. "Not a chance."

Liam didn't need the reassurance because Troy spoke the truth. They were in it for the long haul. Comfortable silence descended, and Liam turned his thoughts to what they were going to do when they arrived at the club. It had been a couple of weeks since they had been there because life had interrupted their usual weekly visit, and he was excited to see his friends again.

It was strange to think that he still didn't know what Dodo looked like outside of his pup suit. He never took his mask off, always staying within his pup role, and his handler never made him. It made Liam wonder if he was hiding or if he was someone high profile who wanted to keep his identity a secret, like Henry had. Either way, it wasn't up to Liam. Dodo had to do what he wanted to do, but it didn't stop Liam from being curious about who he was.

Troy parked in The Den's car park, and they entered the club, signing in and climbing the stairs. They visited the bathroom first so Liam could change into his pup suit. It hadn't been his first choice of changing rooms, but he hadn't wanted to waste time by going home first. As soon as he was ready, they entered the play area, the sound of skin on skin and moans already peaking in the area surrounding the mosh pit.

Nomad came racing over the moment Liam dropped to his knees, and Liam swiped at him.

"Barney, present."

Just like that, Barney stopped and rose, waiting for Master's orders. His ears picked up soft growls and whines, and it was all he could do to stop his head from swivelling around to see what was happening. Master leaned down and fastened the collar around his neck, and Barney whined in response. He'd forgotten about it.

"Good boy, Barney." Master stroked his head. "Okay, go play."

Barney's muscles tensed and, within seconds, was off like a shot. He scampered across the floor towards Nomad, almost bowling the pup over, but Nomad was used to his manoeuvres and evaded him, but it set them on a chase around the area. Barney bounced forward and back on his paws, wanting Nomad to react, but Nomad stayed still, chest to the floor, tail wagging until Barney bounced forward again. Then Nomad did the same and they collided, rolling on the floor as each tried to get on top of the other. He wasn't sure how long he played for, but suddenly balls flew in all directions, taking Barney's attention from his friend.

Changing direction, he raced after a bouncy ball and crashed into a wall when he didn't see it in time. He shook his head, dazed, and Master came over, crouching in front of him.

"Oh, Barney!" Master sighed. "Are you okay?" He rubbed his hand over Barney's head, and Barney whined, nudging at Master's hand.

Master sat on the floor, crossing his legs, and Barney dropped his head into his lap. He closed his eyes and breathed while Master's hands checked him over.

"I don't feel anything worrisome. I need you to talk to me now. How is your head?"

Barney didn't want to let go of his pup space, especially so abruptly, but his master's voice brooked no argument. Liam slipped forward, taking over, and winced.

"I think," he cleared his throat, "I just have an ache. It doesn't seem like anything else is wrong."

"Let's take your mask off for a moment so I can check."

Liam lifted his head so Troy could work, and the cool air hitting his sweaty skin eased the ache a little. Troy slid his fingertips over every inch of Liam's head, checking for bumps, but there was nothing.

Troy chuckled. "Silly pup." He rubbed at Liam's shoulder. "If you're sure. Do you want to play some more?"

"Yes, please."

"Okay, but you must keep track of how you feel. If you feel dizzy or wobbly or anything like that, come to me immediately. That's an order."

"Yes, Sir."

Troy helped him replace the mask, and Barney scrambled up. "Be careful this time."

Barney yipped and wandered off. His head ached, but not enough for him to miss his play time with Nomad and Dodo, who had arrived while Barney had been checked over. He nudged his nose against Dodo, who returned the gesture, and then they set about playing until Master called him for a snack.

As Barney ate and drank, Liam rose to the surface again. He loved everything about his life at that moment. He had a family that was slowly expanding, friends that were becoming more like family, and a boyfriend who would hopefully become more sooner rather than later. Not that he was going to push too quickly. He'd made that mistake before. He couldn't believe how far he'd come since his parents had died. Never expecting to leave Windsor in the first place, his journey had taken him to cities, towns and villages all over the country, but he'd ended up right back where he had been, finding the man he wanted to spend his life with in the town he'd been born in. What were the chances of that?

He'd only known Troy officially for just over four months, but he could imagine his future centred around the man. It was too early to mention moving in together or marrying, but the idea didn't scare Liam as it had once. In fact, he wanted it desperately. He would wait for Troy's clue before he did anything drastic, but one day, he would ask Troy to marry him.

There was no chance he would ever let the man go.

Troy was his. Liam was Troy's.

End of the story.

Or rather, the beginning of *their* story.

• • • • • • • • • •

Read on for a teaser of Secretive Royal, the second book in the Club Royal series and another pet play book. Find out what it takes for Prince Henry to feel secure enough to be himself as a pup, and how Robert helps him.

And you receive a free short story if you sign up to my newsletter: https://elouiseeast.com/newsletter

Secretive Royal Teaser

Henry

"I need to order some flowers to send to Arthur and Isla," his mother said the following day.

"You have an entire garden full of flowers, my dear. Why do you need to buy some?" his father, Patrick Senior, asked.

After crawling out of bed at eleven o'clock, Henry met his mother and father for lunch. His brother, Patrick Junior, had already left for a royal event, and Mary, his sister, was off with her husband and four children at the park, his mother told him.

Victoria's words registered finally, and Henry lifted his head. "I can get some for you, Mother."

She raised her eyebrows. "Are you sure, sweetheart? I can get one of the staff members to do it."

"I don't mind at all. I don't have any plans today."

His mother smiled at him and patted his cheek. "That would be lovely. Thank you, darling. See, honey. Henry understands. The flowers in my garden are for us to look at. If I used my flowers to give to others, I'd have none left. That might make me selfish, but I love my flowers."

Henry stared at his plate as his stomach completed several somersaults. Why had he offered to get the flowers? *Don't be stupid, Henry. You know exactly why?* He took a bite and chewed, tasting nothing; his mind was already on his destination. A stalker he was not, but he had driven past the flower shop several times in passing over the last few days. Not that he'd seen anyone.

The meal finished, and he told Victoria he would fetch the flowers now and bring them back so someone could deliver them. Henry dashed through the hallways to his rooms, changed his shirt and tried to tame his hair. The sides were easy enough because he shaved them, but the top was longer and had an annoying curl in the front if he didn't glue it down. When it finally did as Henry told it to, he locked his room and headed to his car.

The journey wouldn't take him over twenty minutes, but that would be twenty minutes of wondering what the hell he was doing. It was a bad idea to have come here without security, but he couldn't change it now. He parked on the street, sliding a beanie onto his head to hide his features, hopefully. The hair taming he had done was pointless, but he figured it would be worth it as long as they did not throw him out of the shop.

Floresco had an old-fashioned look about it from the brickwork, but the window displays and signage showed how fun and current it was. He stepped inside, a ding of a bell sounding in the back somewhere, and inhaled, closing his eyes.

"Can I help you?"

A woman he recognised from the children's event stood at the counter, her head tilted, eyes squinting.

"Yes. I'd like a bouquet."

"Okay." She glanced over her shoulder. "Do you know what flowers you would like in it?"

"It's to congratulate someone on their pregnancy. Nothing too overwhelming, though they are past their first trimester, so that might not matter now."

"Let me see what I have in the back. Bear with me."

The woman disappeared, and Henry pulled his shaky hands from his pockets. The layout of the shop was of similar design to many. Shelves and shelves with buckets and buckets of flowers on display in every shape and colour he could imagine. On the wall hung paintings of flowers in various locations. In the glass by the counter, there were accessories to go with bouquets and various other trinkets for sale.

Henry crouched to see what was there and had his nose close to the glass display when someone called his name.

"Prince Henry, to what do I owe the pleasure?"

He rose to stand, threading his fingers together to minimise the trembling. "I'd like a pregnancy bouquet, please." He kept his voice steady, though his whole body shook as he locked gazes with Robert.

Robert lifted his chin and narrowed his eyes. "Don't you usually have other people do your errands for you?" Despite his words, he rounded the counter and headed for some purple chrysanthemums.

"We do, but my mother asked me to do this personally." Not quite the truth, but no one will tell. "It's for a family member."

"Fair enough. How many flowers would you like?"

Henry didn't have a clue. "However many you think would be appropriate."

Robert glanced at him again, then bustled around the shop, gathering flowers. Henry watched him, fascinated by the way he moved. He wore a bright blue silk shirt with a black bow at the neck, tight black jeans and black boots with a small heel. A gentle clinking sounded as he moved, coming from the many coloured bangles on his wrists, and he had long earrings that reached his shoulders. All of that was fascinating, but it was his face that had captured Henry's interest again. Flawless skin, rosy cheeks, a deep purple eyeshadow and glossy lips made a face that was born to break hearts.

Henry blinked when he realised Robert had said something. "Sorry. I missed that."

• • • • • • • • • •

Grab it here: https://books2read.com/secretiveroyal

Books by Elouise East

Illuminate Matchmaking
Ignite
Blaze
Kindle
Scorch

Club Royal
Royal Firsts
Rogue Royal
Secretive Royal
Grieving Royal
Disowned Royal
Trained Royal
Awakened Royal
Commanding Royal

Boys, Daddies, Snuggles & More

ELOUISE EAST

Need Him
Trust Him

Daddy
Love Me, Daddy
Soothe Me, Daddy
Spoil Me, Daddy
The Complete Daddy Collection

Love in Flames
Out of the Frying Pan
Smokescreen
Breathing Fire
Love in Flames Collection

Crush
Love Conquers
Instant Desire
Primary Seduction
Deep Down
A Crush for Christmas
Life Support
Covert Strength
Love Scene
Lawful Attraction
Crush Collection Volume 1
Crush Collection Volume 2
Crush Collection Volume 3

Just A Little Crush

First Kiss
He's Behind You
A Special Love

Standalone
Treehouse Whispers
Star-Crossed
Protecting the Thief
Sizzling Chauffeur

<u>**Elouise R East (taboo)**</u>
Dark & Divergent
Forbidden Temptation
Too Many Secrets

Collide
When Fantasies Collide
When Dreams Collide
When Pleasures Collide
When Cravings Collide

ABOUT ELOUISE EAST

Elouise East writes sweet and steamy connections in gay romance. She also touches on taboo stories under the name Elouise R East.

Books that tell the stories where friendship and family are the focal point - be it blood family or chosen - are very important to her. That's why she includes a variety of personalities, talents, ages, situations and abilities as she believes a story or character needs. She wants her characters to be real, to be relatable, to be free to have whatever views they tell her they have. And trust her, most of the time, she does not have *any* say in the matter!

Her characters come to life on the page for her as well as her readers. Their stories unfold in front of her as she writes, and she has very little input into how they want to be shown. Just like real life, the lives of her characters change with every choice, every interaction and every conversation. And she wouldn't have it any other way.

She writes books that are emotionally realistic, even if liberties are taken with other aspects of the stories. She doesn't know any other way to write. It comes from deep inside.

Who is she? A single parent to two children living in the UK. An avid reader who still tries to devour every book she can get her hands on. A student of learning about any subject that takes her fancy. An author of books she would read herself. And a romantic at heart who loves anything cheesy.

Who's joining her on her journey?

Stalk her here... ;-)
Website : https://elouiseeast.com
Newsletter : https://elouiseeast.com/newsletter
All links : https://elouiseeast.com/links